"Is that what this is for you, Ana? Just another job? Because this case is definitely a lot more personal to me."

Benning maneuvered around the counter, and his bare chest nearly pressed against her arm. He set his hand over hers, her quick gasp searing through him. Her warmth penetrated past skin and muscle, deep into his bones. "After what you told me about the Samantha Davis case, I realize now how hard it must've been for you to come back here, and you're standing there as if none of it affects you. But is that how you really feel?"

He wanted—no, needed—to know. Was this going to play out exactly as it had between them the last time? Had he made a mistake requesting her to work this case?

Her mouth parted. "I..."

Skimming his fingers along the back of her hand, he trailed a path up her arm to her jaw, and all of his thoughts burned away. There was only the two of them...

MIDNIGHT ABDUCTION

Nichole Severn

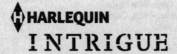

HARLEQUIN
INTRIGUE

I have enough self-awareness to know I worked damn hard on
this book, so I'm dedicating it to me.

Special thanks and acknowledgment are given to Nichole Severn
for her contribution to the Tactical Crime Division miniseries.

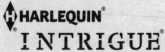

Recycling programs
for this product may
not exist in your area.

ISBN-13: 978-1-335-13652-7

Midnight Abduction

Harlequin Enterprises ULC
22 Adelaide St. West, 40th Floor
Toronto, Ontario M5H 4E3, Canada
www.Harlequin.com

Printed in U.S.A.

Nichole Severn writes explosive romantic suspense with strong heroines, heroes who dare challenge them and a hell of a lot of guns. She resides with her very supportive and patient husband, as well as her demon spawn, in Utah. When she's not writing, she's constantly injuring herself running, rock climbing, practicing yoga and snowboarding. She loves hearing from readers through her website, www.nicholesevern.com, and on Twitter, @nicholesevern.

Books by Nichole Severn

Harlequin Intrigue

Rules in Blackmail
Rules in Rescue
Rules in Deceit
Rules in Defiance

Midnight Abduction

Visit the Author Profile page at Harlequin.com.

CAST OF CHARACTERS

Ana Sofia Ramirez—She's out for redemption. Recruited by the Tactical Crime Division's director from the Bureau's missing-persons' division after her last case ended with a dead victim, she's more determined than ever to recover Benning Reeves's son.

Benning Reeves—Single father and small-town building inspector who's come across evidence of a murder hidden on one of his construction sites; the cost of discovery has led to the kidnapping of his six-year-old twins.

Olivia and Owen Reeves—Benning's six-year-old twins.

Evan Duran—Tactical Crime Division's hostage negotiator, who's fully invested in recovering Benning Reeves's son due to his own dark past of losing his sister as a child.

JC Cantrell—Tactical Crime Division's tactical-operations specialist, who's good at planting bugs, leading surveillance ops or coming up with a ruse to distract someone.

Tactical Crime Division—Rapid-deployment team of FBI agents specializing in hostage negotiation, missing persons, IT, profiling, shootings and terrorism with Director Jill Pembrook at the head.

Prologue

They warned him not to go to the police.

He couldn't think. Couldn't breathe.

Forcing one foot in front of the other, he tried to ignore the gut-wrenching pain at the base of his skull where the kidnapper had slammed him into his kitchen floor and knocked him unconscious. Owen. Olivia. They were out there. Alone. Scared. He hadn't been strong enough to protect them, but he wasn't going to stop trying to find them. Not until he got them back.

A wave of dizziness tilted the world on its axis, and he collided with a wooden street pole. Shoulder-length hair blocked his vision as he fought to regain balance. He'd woken up a little less than fifteen minutes ago, started chasing after the taillights of the SUV as it'd sped down the unpaved road leading into town. He could still taste the dirt in his mouth. They couldn't have gotten far. Someone had to have seen something...

Humidity settled deep into his lungs despite the

dropping temperatures, sweat beading at his temples as he pushed himself upright. Moonlight beamed down on him, exhaustion pulling at every muscle in his body, but he had to keep going. He had to find his kids. They were all he had left. All that mattered.

Colorless, worn mom-and-pop stores lining the town's main street blurred in his vision.

A small group of teenagers—at least what looked like teenagers—gathered around a single point on the sidewalk ahead. The kidnapper had sped into town from his property just on the outskirts, and there were only so many roads that would get the bastard out. Maybe someone in the group could point him in the right direction. He latched on to a kid brushing past him by the collar. "Did you see a black SUV speed through here?"

The boy—sixteen, seventeen—shook his head and pulled away. "Get off me, man."

The echo of voices pierced through the ringing in his ears as the circle of teens closed in on itself in front of Sevierville's oldest hardware store. His lungs burned with shallow breaths as he searched the streets from his position in the middle of the sidewalk. Someone had to have seen something. Anything. He needed—

"She's bleeding!" a girl said. "Someone call for an ambulance!"

The hairs on the back of his neck stood on end. Someone had been hurt? Pushing through the circle of onlookers, he caught sight of pink pajama pants and bright purple toenails. He surrendered to the panic as recognition flared. His heart threatened to burst straight out of his chest as he lunged for the unconscious six-year-old girl sprawled across the pavement. Pain shot through his knees as he scooped her into his arms. "Olivia!"

Chapter One

"Congratulations, Ramirez." Director Jill Pembrook swiped her index finger across the tablet's screen in her hands, and the entire network of monitors embedded into the conference table came to life. "You've got your next assignment."

A new case? It had been so long she was starting to think her past mistakes had caught up with her and negatively impacted her profile with the team. Agent Ana Sofia Ramirez bit back her smile as exaggerated congratulations and clapping from two other agents on the team filled the conference room. Her leather chair groaned as she leaned back to study the main screen behind the director, her fingernails skimming the table's surface. "What's the case?"

"Abduction of a six-year-old boy," the director said.

The room quieted, the silence almost a physical presence as the tendons between Ana's shoulders and neck tightened. Drawing a deep breath, she focused on the monitor in front of her. This was what she'd been trained for—finding the missing—but not a single agent around this table would volunteer for an assignment like this. "Timeline?"

"We've been given twenty-four hours. The father is adamant no one but the agent he requested can get involved in the recovery, but the clock is already ticking, and we're going to use all available resources we have whether he likes it or not. That's where you come in." Director Pembrook turned to the largest screen at the head of the conference room, pulling up a map pinpointing a small section of private property a little outside Sevierville, TN. The petite, graying woman with sharp features at the head of the room had been a force to be reckoned with within the Bureau for nearly forty years. She wasn't a woman to disappoint, and Ana didn't plan on testing that theory. The director tossed a manila envelope across the table. "You'll go undercover as a former lover who's in town visiting and has heard the devastating news his son has been taken. I want you to get close to the father and find out what he could possibly gain from this abduction by keeping us in the dark. Agents Cantrell and Duran will provide support from this location until you say otherwise."

Maldicion. Damn it.

"If this is a targeted abduction, the kidnappers will have done their research. They might've already sifted through the people in the boy's life." Ana lifted her gaze to the men across the table from her. Agent JC Cantrell handled surveillance, Evan Duran worked hostage negotiations and Ana did whatever it took to find the missing. Together they made up only part of the Tactical Crime Division, and it looked like they were headed to Sevierville, TN, the last place she'd intended to set foot again. Too many memories. Too much pain. But the thought of passing on this case, when she'd battled so hard to make up for the past, built pressure behind her sternum. "What's the guarantee my cover won't be blown the instant I come into contact?"

"That won't be a problem during this investigation," Director Pembrook said.

While the FBI had massive resources and vast intelligence relating to criminal activity, they were headquartered in DC. The Bureau had regional field offices in major cities across the country to assist local police when needed, but that left smaller or rural towns with sparse populations without rapid support. More and more, agents and federal law agencies mobilized to remote locations to address large-scale crime scenes and criminal activity. Terrorism, hostage situations, kidnappings, shootings. But with the growing concern and need for ever-increasing response times to these criminal events, the Bureau saw the need for a specialized tech and tactical team, combining specialists from several active units. Together they made up Tactical Crime Division.

"How long has the boy been missing?" As one of the most successful hostage negotiators in Bureau history, Agent Evan Duran saved hundreds of lives over the course of his career by getting more information out of a suspect with as little commitment as possible on his part. If the kidnappers had made any kind of demand, Ana trusted him to mine for the intel she needed to find the victim. "Any demands?"

"Six hours." Director Pembrook took her seat at the head of the table. "And, no."

"There hasn't been a ransom call?" Ana swiped through the file directly from the monitor in front of her. Every forty seconds a child went missing somewhere in the United States. More than 460,000 children were reported missing each year. Of those missing children, almost 1,500 of them had been kidnapped, with most of those reports narrowing the suspect list to a parent or close relative as the abductor. There was a chance the boy's mother was responsible, which would account for the lack of demands or ransom. Or… Ana froze, paralyzed as she read the father's name on the police report. "Benning Reeves."

The boy who'd been kidnapped was Benning's son, Owen.

"He asked for you specifically, Ramirez." The weight of Director Pembrook's attention crushed the air from her lungs. She was the agent Benning had requested. Was that why she'd been given the lead on this case? Not because of her experience in recovering the missing but because she'd actually been intimate with the man keeping the FBI at arm's length during his son's kidnapping investigation.

The director was right. Her cover wouldn't be a problem during the investigation.

It was the truth.

Ana swiped her tongue between dry lips. "What about the girl? Olivia."

"She was taken, too, but local police recovered her minutes after the abduction." Relief coursed through her as the director's gaze narrowed, but Ana didn't have time to crumble under the pressure of Pembrook's study. Someone out there had taken Benning's son, and time was running out to get him back. The question was why. As far as she knew, Benning had kept his job as a building inspector for the city all these years, wasn't in debt and wasn't the kind of man to get himself mixed up in criminal activity. Assuming this was personal, why would someone target Benning through his children? "They believe she escaped her kidnapper's vehicle while in motion, but it's impossible to know for sure until her medical team lets law enforcement interview her. You need to be there when she wakes up and find out what she remembers to help recover the son. Whether the father wants the TCD officially involved or not."

She nodded. They could at least exclude the twins' mother from their list of suspects. Lilly Reeves had passed away giving birth to them six years ago. Ana struggled to control the racing pulse at the base of her skull. Benning had asked for her help with this case, but given the last time they'd been in the same room—the same bed—she didn't understand why. A single phone call had changed everything between them, and he'd moved on. He'd married a woman in town and had children not long after Ana had left. Now she was expected to reinsert herself back into his life in order to find his missing son.

There were far more qualified agents to handle this investigation, agents who hadn't put their entire career at risk because of one wrong decision. Agents who didn't have a personal connection to the case. What was she supposed to say to him after all these years? They hadn't spoken since that night, despite the small part of her that'd urged her to reach out, to reconnect with the only person she just couldn't seem to detach herself from. She swallowed through the tightness in her throat. No matter what'd happened between her and Benning, she couldn't let emotion cloud her judgment this time. A little boy's life was at risk.

"I'll look into the traffic cameras." Agent JC Cantrell shoved to his feet, locking light green eyes on her as he stood. Specializing in surveillance operations, the former soldier led most of TCD's surveillance ops, but whether those ops were completely legal was another question. Right now Ana didn't care. There was a six-year-old boy out there—alone and afraid. This was what their division had been trained for, what she'd been trained for. She wouldn't make the same mistake with this case as she had when Benning had been in her life the first time. JC headed for the door, Duran at his side. "With any kind of luck, I'll have a license plate for you and a location of the getaway vehicle in the next hour."

"Keep me in the loop and stay close to your phones. I'll call you if I need you." Ana pushed away from the conference table to stand, her long, dark hair inherited from her Hispanic father sliding over her shoulder in front of her. Sevierville wasn't far, only thirty miles southeast of TCD headquarters here in Knoxville, but if she wanted to interview Benning's daughter before the girl's medical team gave permission to local PD, she had to leave now. With a nod toward Director Pembrook, she pushed her chair into the edge of the table. "I'll brief you as soon as I'm finished interviewing Olivia Benning."

"Be careful, Ramirez." The director's voice carried across the conference room, stopping Ana in her escape toward the double glass doors. The weight of those steel-gray eyes drilled straight through her. "I assigned you this case because you have a connection to the victim's father and he's made it clear he won't play nice with anyone else, but don't let your emotions and that connection get in the way of doing your job." Pembrook's voice softened. "We can't afford to lose anyone else. Understand?"

The hairs on the back of her neck stood on end, but she couldn't turn around. She couldn't face the reality of Jill Pembrook's warning. Gravity increased its natural pull on her body. The backs of her knees shook as a fresh wave of memories penetrated the barrier she'd built over the past seven years. She curled her fingernails into the centers of her palms, and just as quickly as they'd charged forward, she closed the lid to the box at the back of her mind. She'd gotten good at that. Compartmentalizing, detaching herself from feeling the things she didn't want to admit to herself. Especially when it came to Benning Reeves. But underneath the numbness and denial, Ana understood the director's advice. Getting Benning's son home to his family would be her last chance to save her career. She'd failed a victim once. She wouldn't let it happen again. "Yes, ma'am."

BENNING REEVES CROSSED the small room for the eighth—or was it the ninth?—time in as many minutes. It'd been almost five hours since he'd woken in the middle of his house, his children gone. And Olivia… He slowed at the side of her hospital bed. Her small body nearly disappeared in the heaping of pillows and blankets he'd packed around her as her chest rose and fell in smooth, rhythmic breaths. The sedative the nurse had given her would keep his daughter unconscious for the next few hours. It was the only way to ensure her brain would get the rest it needed. He smoothed her short brunette hair away from her face. Truth was, the doctors had no idea if her memories would come back. Something about trauma-induced amnesia. Dissociative? She'd barely remembered her brother's name when she'd been questioned, let alone what'd happened to him after she'd escaped the SUV.

Tremors racked through his hand, and he forced himself to back away for fear of waking her. The kidnapper should've made contact by now, given him further instructions or proof of life. His ears rang. He needed to be out there looking for his son, but he didn't dare leave Olivia here on her own, either. Not after what she'd been through. Heat built in his chest. Someone had broken into his home, knocked him unconscious and taken his children. All because of what'd he found on that construction site.

The fire spread under his skin, and he closed his eyes as the all-too-familiar feeling of instability he'd kept in check all these years clawed for release. Benning unpocketed his phone, the sight of the photo behind the shattered glass immediately drowning the ringing in his ears. His pulse evened as he studied his twins' smiling faces as they tackled him from behind on the screen. He'd get Owen back. He'd already lost too many people in his life. He couldn't lose his kids, too.

A surge of awareness hiked his senses into overdrive, and Benning followed it to the hospital room door. Brown eyes ringed with green centered on him, and the world dropped out from under him. She'd come. In the minutes following Olivia's arrival at the hospital, he hadn't known who else to call. Or if she'd come back to Sevierville. The kidnapper had warned him not to involve law enforcement before knocking him unconscious, but Ana Sofia Ramirez wasn't just a federal agent. She'd been everything to him. Before she'd ripped his heart from his chest in the middle of the night without warning.

Her flawless Hispanic heritage intensified the angles of her cheekbones and nose, silky dark hair reflecting the fluorescent lighting from above, just as he remembered. Pressure built behind his sternum—had been for the past seven years—and he wanted nothing more than to close the distance between them in an attempt to release it. "Ana."

"I came as soon as I heard the news." She rushed toward him and dropped a duffel bag at her feet. Wrapping her arms around his waist, the woman who'd walked out of his life melted into him, and everything inside him quieted in an instant. The insecurity, the rage, the fear and the failure. Now there was only calm. Clarity. Hints of her perfume—something light and fresh—tickled the back of his throat as he buried his nose against the crown of her head. At five foot five, she fit perfectly against him. Toward the end of their relationship, he'd even believed she'd been made specifically for him. Skimming her chin along his shoulder, she set her mouth at his ear, eliciting a shudder from his spine, and lowered her voice. "The kidnapper could be listening. Pretend we're two friends randomly coming back into contact, and my team and I will do whatever it takes to get your son back."

His insides tightened. Right. Her team. The hug

hadn't been personal, simply a way to get her message across. She hadn't come because he'd called in a personal favor. She'd come to do her job. But given the fact his kids had been targeted in order to get to him, he'd do whatever the hell she instructed. He just wanted his son back. No matter the cost. He increased the space between them, shutting down the internal reaction to her proximity exploding through him, and cleared his throat. "What are you doing here?"

"It's my parents' fortieth wedding anniversary. My brothers and I are flying in to surprise them, but then I heard about what happened, and I wanted to make sure you were okay." Weaving truth in with the lie. He'd read about that, how law enforcement officials, especially those assigned undercover work, trained to remember their stories by inserting bits and pieces of their own lives into their cover stories. Ana did have brothers. Three of them. But as for the wedding anniversary and wanting to check up on him, Benning was sure she'd improvised. Ana pulled her hair back in a tie and turned toward Olivia still asleep in the bed. Her knees popped as she crouched to unzip the duffel she'd brought. In his next breath she straightened with a small black box in her hand and moved toward the bed with the device raised out in front of her. Pulses of green light strengthened on the screen as she moved around the room. "How is she? Any news about Owen?"

She believed the kidnapper was listening. That

was what she'd said. Waiting for him to see if he'd call the police? But unless the man who'd broken into his home knew Olivia would escape the SUV and which hospital room she'd be assigned when she arrived, Benning didn't see how it was possible after Olivia had been checked in. He'd been by her bedside the entire time, only her nurses and doctors coming in and out of the room. "Nothing yet. Olivia suffered a concussion when she escaped the SUV. Doctors aren't sure if the damage goes deeper than her short-term memory, but they'll—"

A red light flashed on the device in Ana's hand, and she stilled. With a quick glance over her shoulder toward him, she reached behind the faux wood headboard of Olivia's bed and detached something from the back. Swinging her hand toward him, she stepped away from his daughter and held out the miniature circle-shaped piece of metal. She extended her index finger of her other hand in a spiral motion to signal him to keep talking.

Someone had installed a bug in his daughter's hospital room. Either they knew she'd wind up in this hospital room or—Benning curled his fingers into tight fists as he ran through a mental list of people who'd stepped foot inside this room—one of the people on Olivia's medical staff had placed the bug while attending to her injuries. He swallowed, tried to keep his voice even as Ana stared up at him. "They'll run more tests once she's awake."

"How are you doing?" She nodded before ma-

neuvering past him to the other side of the room.
Dropping the bug into the glass of water at Oliva's
bedside, she searched the rest of the room, not seemingly interested in his answer.

"It's been a long night," he said.

The light on her detector remained green. Physical relief smoothed her expression as she pocketed
the black box into her knee-length coat when she
was finished, and a hint of the woman he remembered returned. "The rest of the room is clear. They
won't be able to hear anything now. I'll be sure to
get the bug to one of the agents on my team. There's
a chance we can trace it back to its owner and find
out who took your son."

And there she was. The federal agent he'd fallen
for the instant she'd walked onto that construction
site seven years ago interviewing anyone on his crew
who might've known about the disappearance of a
local teenage girl. Benning latched on to the hand-
rail of his daughter's hospital bed in an attempt to
keep himself in the moment. "Assuming the man
who took him is the same one who planted that bug."

But what were the chances the two weren't connected?

"Yes." She nodded toward him, her voice flat, un-
emotional, and his gut clenched. "You're bleeding.
Has someone looked at that cut on the back of your
head? I can stay with her—"

"I'm fine." It was a lie, but he wasn't about to
leave Olivia's side. She'd already been through so

much; he didn't want her waking up without him in the room. He tracked Ana's every move with an awareness he hadn't experienced since the night she'd left Sevierville all those years ago, noted the slight bulge beneath the left side of her jacket. Her service weapon. He'd imagined confronting her so many times, memorized what he'd say, how she'd react. None of it included him asking for her help, her armed with a gun or one of his children missing.

She'd made her choice. She'd decided her career was more important than what they could have together and had run off to save the world. He'd stayed here, and in the wake of losing her, he'd made the stupidest mistake of his life. He'd rebounded. When Lilly told him about the pregnancy, he'd married her, worked at building a real family together for the sake of their twins, despite the lack of love between them. It'd been nothing more than a one-night fling the night he and his late wife had gotten together, but that one night had changed the course of his life. Benning tucked his hands in his jeans. "Ana, I know why you left, but—"

"All that matters right now is getting your son back." Moving around the end of the bed, she hauled the duffel bag into an empty chair, her bangs hiding the dark shadows in her eyes. "That's why you requested me to work this case, isn't it? This is what I do."

Right. He'd read the articles splashed on the front page of *The Mountain Press*, watched the interviews on the major news channels. According to the media, her recovery rates were the highest in the Bureau. When it came to finding the missing, Agent Ana Sofia Ramirez was the best. Right now he needed the best to find his son. He'd shut down the urge to reach out to her over the years, telling himself she'd left for a reason and he was the last person she wanted to hear from, but as far as he was concerned, she would always be unfinished business. "The guy who broke into my house, the one who took my son. I think he's tied to one of the construction sites I inspected—"

A red dot centered over her heart, and Benning lunged.

A gunshot exploded overhead.

Broken glass hit the bottom of Olivia's bed and sliced across the exposed skin of his arm. Pain shot up his wrists as they landed hard on the cold tile. Her sharp exhale rushed across the sensitive skin under his chin and beard, and his heart shot into his throat.

Rolling him off her, Ana pushed to a crouch, her service weapon already in hand.

A familiar scream pierced through the settling silence.

"Olivia." He crawled toward the bed, trying to keep as low as possible. Sunlight reflected off bright blue eyes matching his own as he leveled his gaze with the mattress, and he wrapped his hand around hers. The bruising along his daughter's wrists and arms had darkened over the past few hours, but even more terrifying: someone had taken a shot at them. "It's okay, baby. I'm here."

"Daddy." Her whisper tore through him.

Ana pressed her back against the wall beside the window, then straightened to crane her head around the windowsill. "We have to get out of here."

"I'm not leaving her." His phone vibrated in his pocket. He extracted his cell as Ana turned hazel-green eyes onto him. The number was blocked. Warning tensed the muscles across his shoulders. This was it, the call he'd been waiting for. Locking his gaze on Ana's, he tapped the screen to answer, then put the call on Speaker. "Who is this?"

"I warned you about involving law enforcement, Mr. Reeves," an unfamiliar voice said. "Now your son is going to pay the price for your mistake."

"Let me talk to him. Let me talk to my son." No answer. Benning tightened his hold on Olivia's hand, his breaths coming shorter and faster. "Let me talk to my son!"

The call ended.

Chapter Two

No payment demand or instructions. No proof of life. Whoever'd taken Benning's son wasn't following typical patterns for an abduction. Which meant this was more than a simple kidnapping. They wanted to hurt Benning, manipulate him. Or they wanted something from him. The question was why.

Ana scoured the parking lot two more times. A gunman couldn't fire a shot into a hospital without exposing himself, but there was no movement. Nothing to give her an idea of who'd pulled the trigger, or if they were still out there. She locked her grip around her weapon and turned toward Benning. Either way they were sitting ducks in this room. "Get her out of the bed. We've got to move."

He shook his head. "Olivia's not going anywhere. She needs rest. Her head—"

"You see these bruises around her wrists? How thin they are?" She closed the distance between her and the side of the bed opposite him. Ana flipped his daughter's hand over as gently as she could. "There's not enough skin damage for them to be caused by a rope or handcuffs. These are from zip ties, Benning. Someone bound her wrists while she was in that SUV, and she tried to get free, but she's not strong enough to get out of them herself."

He took a step back. "What are you saying?"

"I'm saying he let her go." She steadied her attention on him, tried to keep the warning out of her voice as much as possible. Benning was a smart man, but sometimes the fear of losing a child hazed over a parent's ability to string reality together. "Whoever took her, whoever took Owen? They wanted Olivia to be found. They wanted you in this room and planted the device we found to ensure you followed whatever instructions they'd given you the first time they contacted you." She studied his expression for any hint she'd hit the nail on the head, and her heart rate spiked as he flinched against the accusation. She was right, and the phone call he'd received seconds ago confirmed it. The kidnapper had warned him not to involve law enforcement, on threat of harming his son, because they weren't finished with Benning. "They knew exactly where to find you. Do you really want to put Olivia's life in more danger by staying here, or do you want to save both your daughter and your son?"

One breath. Two. Benning grabbed the near-empty IV bag, then scooped his daughter gently into his arms. Olivia's small body fell limp against his muscled chest as she continued to combat whatever sedative her doctors had put in that IV. He rounded the end of the bed, those bright blue eyes settling on her. Warmth shot up her neck and into her face as the veins in his sinewy arms fought to break through skin. He hadn't changed much over the years since she'd last seen him, but there was a new roughness to him, a strength that hadn't been there before and she couldn't look away. "Do whatever it takes to get her out of here. Okay? She's the only one who matters."

"I'll get you both out of here. I give you my word." The adrenaline rush increased her focus. She'd memorized the layout of the hospital before she'd left Knoxville. There were three exits from the second floor, not including the windows, but they'd take the stairs at the back of the building in case the shooter had stuck around. She headed toward the door and intercepted his path into the hallway. Adjusting her grip on her weapon, she pulled open the door a crack and studied both ends of the hallway. Lucky for them, Olivia's room was positioned in the corner, the closest to the stairs. Somehow, her kidnapper had gotten access, left the listening device and escaped without notice. Which meant they weren't dealing with an amateur. "Stay behind me. Use me as a shield if you have to."

"Okay." His voice dropped into graveled territory, as though he was fighting to keep the inflection out of his words.

She twisted her chin directly over one shoulder. "As soon as we're safe, you're going to tell me why someone would target your kids to get to you and who exactly was on the other end of that phone call." Because unless he trusted her, his son might not make it home alive.

She moved into the hallway, shouts hiking her nerves into overdrive. The officers assigned to sit on Olivia Reeves until she woke up would've heard the gunshot, but she and Benning couldn't wait around to give their statements. There was no telling how far the abductor would go to ensure they weren't connected to attempted murder and kidnapping charges. Or how many people they'd hurt along the way. She cleared the hallway, the lights reflecting off the white tile bright. Nodding toward the exit to their left, she maneuvered Benning and Olivia past her. "Stairs."

She followed close on his heels through the door as uniforms came around the corner down the hall. Carefully closing the stairwell door behind them, they descended the stairs and pushed through the maintenance exit on the first floor until crisp winter air brushed across the exposed skin of her neck. Swinging her weapon up, she swept the parking lot. No movement. Nothing to suggest an ambush, but she wouldn't let her guard down until Benning and his daughter were safe. "Black SUV five stalls back. Go."

They crossed the parking lot at a jog, but every cell in her body screamed warning as movement registered off to her left. She had only a moment to react. Ana shoved Benning and Olivia behind the nearest car with everything she had. Gunfire ripped across the asphalt. A bullet cut through the thick fabric of her coat as she fired back at the masked shooter taking cover behind a vehicle two rows over. Once. Twice. Olivia's scream pierced through the thud of her pulse behind her ears, but Ana couldn't focus on that right now. Both hands around her weapon, she centered herself behind a parked vehicle between her and the shooter and pulled the trigger three more times, but it was too late. The shooter was already climbing behind the wheel of a black SUV. Maybe even the same vehicle used to abduct Owen and Olivia. In the span of two breaths, he fishtailed out of the parking lot and disappeared down the street.

Hijo de...

"I think it's safe to say my cover is blown." Her exhales crystallized in front of her mouth as she turned back toward Benning and his daughter, the girl's hands locked over her ears. Her fingers tingled with the urge to comfort the six-year-old, but Ana chose to reholster her weapon and positioned her coat over the fresh wound in her side before Olivia saw the blood. The girl had already suffered so much. She didn't need more material for her nightmares. "Let's get her in the car. We can't wait around for the shooter to come back and finish the job."

Hauling Olivia into his chest, Benning straightened and secured his daughter in the back seat of the SUV. His mountainous shoulders and arms were massive compared to the girl's small frame as he brushed something from Olivia's chin, his whisper inaudible to Ana less than two feet away. He was careful of his daughter's injuries, caring, and Ana fought against the sudden tightness in her throat. There'd been a time she'd imagined him treating their future children's scrapes and bruises like he'd done with Olivia. Her throat threatened to close, and she turned away from the visual to dislodge the string of thought. She'd buried that future the second she'd snuck out of his room that night.

"Are you okay?" Benning closed the door, his focus on Ana, and her entire body heated as though he'd physically trailed a path down across her clavicle bone. He closed the small distance between them, reaching out, but she dodged his attempt to touch her. His expression fell, his hand falling to his side. "I thought you'd been hit."

"I'm fine." Lie. The pain crushed the air from her lungs. She'd most likely need stitches—maybe a surgeon—but she couldn't worry about that right now. They were vulnerable out here in the open. Targets. Blood trickled into the waistband of her slacks, the ache the only thing keeping her in the moment. He had every reason to hate her for what she'd done, but right now the way he looked at her, as though she were the only woman in the entire world, weighed heavy on her chest.

It'd be so easy to fall back into old habits with him, to remember the way his entire face lit up when she walked into a room, the promises of forever he'd whispered into her ear from between the sheets, how happy they'd been simply curled up in front of the fireplace. It'd be easy to become attached to the man she'd walked away from, but she'd come back to Sevierville for one thing: to find Owen Reeves.

She couldn't do that without the truth.

Ana clamped her hand to her side, awakening her pain receptors all over again, and wrenched open the driver-side door. Every minute they wasted out here was another minute Owen was in the hands of his kidnapper. She wanted to bring him home. *Needed* to. "Get in."

Benning rounded the back of the SUV as she settled into the front and pushed the ignition button to start the engine. The interior filled with his wild, pine-and-dirt scent as he climbed inside, and she breathed a bit deeper, held on to it as much as she could in an attempt to dull the pain in her side. She'd missed that smell, a combination of soap and outdoors. Missed him.

"You can't go back to your house. The shooter could be waiting for you there." She maneuvered the SUV out of the hospital parking lot as sirens echoed down the street. The officers who'd been stationed to watch Olivia had called in backup, and while Owen Reeves's kidnapping fell under federal jurisdiction, they'd need all the help they could get. Ana hit the call button on the steering wheel, the line connecting almost instantly.

"Calling for help already?" JC asked. "This

wouldn't be about Sevierville PD reporting shots fired at LeConte Medical Center, would it?"

"You read my mind. We've got an unknown shooter in a black SUV, no plates and local PD closing in on the scene." She pressed her foot against the accelerator, the weight of Benning's attention increasing as they sped from the hospital. "Think you could take care of that for me?"

"I live to serve." JC's laugh fought to lighten the tension tightening down her back, but Ana had a feeling that as long as Benning was involved, nothing would help. "I checked the traffic cams around the time of the kidnapping. There's no sign of the getaway vehicle. I've got IT working their magic, but someone brought down the cameras beforehand or knew where they were positioned so they could stay clear. We've got nothing."

Which meant the kidnapping had been premeditated. This was the work of a professional.

Benning ran one hand through his hair, leveraging his elbow on the passenger-side door. Frustration played clearly across his expression, and in that moment her instincts said there was more to this investigation than a simple kidnapping.

"Thanks, JC. Sevierville PD is about to bag a listening device I found attached to the back of the girl's hospital bed. I need you to see if you can trace it back to its owner. Call me if you find something." She ended the call, checked the rearview mirror for any vehicles behind them, then slammed her foot against the brakes. The seat belt pressed into her chest as her body weight shifted forward from momentum.

"What are you doing?" Benning straightened, braced against the dashboard. Pushing his dark, shoulder-length hair behind one ear, he turned on her. "The shooter could be following us."

"You brought me into this investigation by requesting me specifically, but I can't do my job if you're keeping information from me. I think now's a good time to tell me who took your son, don't you?" Heated rubber filled her lungs, clearing his scent from her system. She faced him. "The kidnapper contacted you before that call in the hospital, didn't he? He warned you not to involve the police, so you thought if you reached out to a former acquaintance who happened to be an FBI agent, he wouldn't know. The listening device, the rifle shot through the window… This guy is a professional, Benning, and he has targeted you. What does he want?"

He stared out the windshield. Seconds ticked by, a minute. Pressure built behind her sternum the longer he took to answer, but when he turned that bright blue gaze to hers, her gut said she wasn't going to like the next words out of his mouth. "He wants the skull I found."

"A HUMAN SKULL?" she asked.

Snowflakes drifted across the windshield. January temperatures tunneled through his shirt, but the memories of what he'd found—evidence of what a killer had done—generated enough heat to haunt him for the rest of his life. Someone had kidnapped his twins and taken a shot at Ana through the window of his daughter's hospital room. Because of him. He couldn't keep the truth to himself any longer. "A woman approached me two weeks ago on the site of one of the buildings I was inspecting. She offered me fifty thousand dollars to give a residential project the go-ahead, but the crew had cut too many corners. There were sections of framing missing. The plumbing wasn't up to code." Benning smoothed his palms down his jeans, blood crusted on the underside of his fingers. Olivia's. Glancing toward his daughter in the back seat, he studied the perfect curve of her mouth as she slept—anything to distract him from the fact he'd almost lost her less than six hours ago. And that her brother had been taken. "I couldn't ignore any of that, so I said no. Told her I suggested she hire a new crew to do the job right before the city came in with a lawsuit."

Ana's uniquely enthralling eyes—the ones he'd dreamed about for years—softened. "What happened after you gave her your answer?"

"I couldn't get past the thought that she'd bribed inspectors before. She seemed…comfortable with the approach, so I started looking into the company's past projects." He shook his head. "I found settlement paperwork between Britland Construction and tenants who'd been injured or left homeless because their buildings weren't up to code. Years' worth, with millions of dollars at stake, but the problems were only getting worse, and somehow their projects kept getting approved by the city. I wanted to know why."

"You started investigating on your own." Ana leaned back in her seat, her expression smooth. How was that possible? How could she pretend nothing had happened between them—that she hadn't torn his life apart—and keep herself so...detached?

"I went to the police. They brought the woman in for questioning, but there wasn't enough evidence to prove Britland had sent her to bribe me. Her lawyer threw around so much weight, the investigating officers couldn't even verify she worked for them. Dozens of families were being hurt every year because of this company's negligence and greed, and I couldn't let them get away with it. I'm the only inspector the city has, so when Britland needed another project across town inspected, I added the job to my afterhours schedule last night. I ripped open one of the main walls to check the electrical." He dug his phone out from his pocket and swiped to a photo he'd hidden in the cloud. "That's when I found this."

Ana took the phone from him, her fingers brushing against his, and everything inside him fired in a heated chain reaction. She'd always had that effect on him; had always been able to take total control of his body with a single touch, but despite the fact he'd been the one to bring her back into his life, he couldn't give in to those feelings now. Now he had to get his family back. That was all that mattered. "That's most definitely a skull." She brought the screen closer to her face. "We won't be able to narrow time or cause of death without my forensics team getting their hands on it, but that hole in the frontal bone looks like a gunshot wound."

He'd thought so, too.

"I called the police as soon as I found it, but before my call connected, someone shouted at me from behind. I turned around to find a gun and a flashlight pointed at my face. I thought the guy was site security, so I explained who I was, and why I was there and offered to show my work order, but when my eyes adjusted, I noticed the ski mask." His heart rate picked up as a fresh wave of adrenaline dumped into his veins. "He said he'd wished I hadn't found the skull, and that he was sorry. He had his finger on the trigger, and I knew then he was going to shoot me for what I'd seen, but then an actual security guard ordered him to lower his weapon. The shooting started, and I just grabbed the skull and ran."

"You said he was wearing a mask. Did you pick up on any other characteristics? Anything we can use to identify him?" she said. "An accent, tattoos, scars, clothing, the color of his eyes?"

"No, none of that." He shook his head.

She handed the phone back, seemingly determined to avoid physical contact this time. "Where's the skull now?"

"Safe." He hit the sleep button on the side of his

phone. "At first, I didn't think Britland could be responsible. It'd be too obvious. There was a paper
trail linking the payoffs to the victims, and the skull
I found had been drywalled inside their own building, but as soon as I left the site, I knew I couldn't go
home. At least not right away, in case the guy in the
mask decided to follow me." Rage burned through
him. He should've been more careful. Should've
taken the skull straight to the police. He cleared his
throat as his eyes burned. "My nanny—Jo West—
was supposed to drop the kids off for a sleepover at
a friend's house, but she called me saying Owen had
been sick for the past few hours, and he wanted me
to come home." Now his nanny was missing. "When
I got to my house, I hid the skull in an old, unfinished brick fireplace my dad had started building
when I was a kid, but when I got inside the bastard
was already in my house. I fought him off as long
as I could, but I couldn't stop him. He hit me from
behind almost the second I walked through the front
door. When I woke up, my phone was vibrating in
my pocket, the house was quiet and Jo and the kids…
They were gone."

Now the SOB had his son.

"He warned me if I involved the FBI or police,
I'd never see my kids again, said I had twenty-four
hours to turn over the skull before he'd start hurting
them." He hadn't been fast enough, strong enough.
But with the evidence he'd recovered, he was going
to expose them all. He'd make sure they never hurt

his family again, never hurt anyone's family again. "I know what I'm asking you to do, Ana. I know you don't want to be here, but these people went after my family. You're the only one who can help me find my son before it's too late."

Pain throbbed at the base of his head in rhythm with his racing heart rate.

"Then it's a good thing I came into town for my parents' surprise wedding anniversary." The hardened exterior she'd hidden behind the moment she'd stepped into his daughter's hospital room cracked as one corner of her mouth lifted into a smile. She put the SUV back in gear and pulled into traffic. "There's a safe house the FBI has secured outside of town. You and Olivia can stay there while I collect your bodiless friend from the fireplace. After that, our forensics unit can run dental and DNA for an identification and hopefully trace the victim back to the kidnapper. If he wants the evidence so badly, there's a reason. I'm going to find out what that reason is so we can get your son back."

Water and snow kicked up alongside the SUV as they headed out of the city, Main Street passing in a blur. In this quiet, Smokey Mountain town of less than 20,000 residents, there wasn't much in the way of scandal and crime, but when it hit, it hit hard and left a wake of grief behind. Plowed streets disappeared under a new layer of snow, the trees growing thicker as they headed southeast along the highway. Oliva's soft snores and the high-pitched clearing of slush beneath the tires coaxed him to relax, but he couldn't ignore the strained silence between him and the woman who'd amazingly put herself in harm's way for his daughter. "Thank you for taking the case. I didn't know who else to call."

"No need to thank me." Thin lines around her eyes deepened as though she was in the middle of an internal battle of some kind. "This is my job. This is what I'm trained for."

Was that all this was to her? A job? His gut clenched. He should've known better; should've realized reaching out to her wasn't going to change anything. He should've had enough sense to let the past die, but he hadn't been able to stop the loop of what-ifs since that morning he'd woken alone in his bed. Until he caught sight of the stain of blood pooling on her slacks. Benning jerked forward in his seat. Hell. She'd gotten shot, her wound had been bleeding this entire time and she'd kept it to herself. "Damn it, Ana, you're hurt. Pull over."

"I said I'm fine. It's been six hours since your son was taken. If we get stuck out here, we're not finding Owen before the deadline." The muscles along her throat worked to swallow. Her left arm hung limp at her side, her free hand gripped so tight around the steering wheel her knuckles threatened to split the translucent skin. "Besides, I've survived a lot worse than a bullet wound. Tell me about Owen."

A lot worse? What the hell did that mean?

Hesitation gripped him hard, but he couldn't argue

with her logic. Every minute they were on the run was another minute his son didn't have. "He hates peanut butter. Won't go near the stuff. All he wants to do is sit on his tablet and watch those stupid videos online of other kids playing with toys, but I let him because it makes him happy." Adrenaline from the shootout at the hospital drained from his veins the longer he talked about Owen. "The kid can't go anywhere without the blanket I bought for him while Lilly was pregnant with them. Sleeps with it every night, takes it with him wherever he goes. Except school. That's where I had to draw the line."

That damn blanket was still right where Owen had left it in the middle of the living room floor during the abduction. His son must've dropped it when the kidnapper had rushed him out the door. Only now Benning wished he would've brought it with him, had something to hold on to of his son's. A minute passed, maybe more.

"I'm sorry about Lilly. I wanted to…reach out, but I wasn't sure after what'd happened between us…" She cleared her throat, redirected her attention out the driver-side window. "Has it been hard? Not having her around?"

He let her words settle, focusing on the topic of his late wife.

"At first." He couldn't really remember single moments of the first few months of the twins' lives. It'd been a blur of diaper changes and spit up, of having to take a leave of absence until he'd found the right nanny to take over, of trying to make sense of being a single father. Of trying to forget about the rookie federal agent who'd extracted herself from his life as quickly as she'd appeared. He studied the snow as it melted against the hood of the SUV. "My entire world got turned upside down. I had to start thinking of things like formula temperature, not being able to sleep for more than an hour at a time and which diapers worked better for girls compared to boys. To be honest, I still don't know what I'm doing or if I'm making the right choices for them." He scratched at the spot of dried mud on his jeans as heat flared into his neck and face. "Guess I should be grateful I got to do any of that stuff... Lilly didn't."

"I'm sorry." Sincerity laced her words. "I didn't mean—"

"No, it's okay." He'd healed from that wound a long time ago. "Lilly and I both knew what we were getting ourselves into, and we'd both accepted the possibility that we might not be able to make it work. We agreed what'd happened between us was a mistake, but I can't say I regret what came out of it. I wouldn't have Owen or Olivia if it wasn't for her." He twisted toward Olivia. "What about you? Got someone waiting for you when you head back to Knoxville?"

The idea she'd found happiness with another man—someone other than him—built pressure behind his sternum, which didn't make sense. She'd been the one to drive the wedge between them.

What she did with her life after that shouldn't have even crossed his mind, but there she'd been, always emerging when he failed to distract himself or had a few minutes alone.

"No. The cases I work, the things I've seen…" Ana shifted in her seat, flinched against an invisible pain he couldn't see. She slowed the SUV on approach to one of the side roads off the highway up ahead. She turned that hazel gaze onto him for a moment as she maneuvered the vehicle up the long, winding drive to a cabin set a little less than an eighth of a mile back on the property. In an instant he was the man completely smitten with the rookie fresh from Quantico who'd been working her first missing persons case in Sevierville. "It's impossible to find the light when I have to spend all my time walking through the dark."

Chapter Three

Trees surrounded the property from every side, cutting them off from civilization. Ana climbed the short set of stairs leading up to a covered porch, old wood protesting under her boots. Nobody would be able to find them out here, and with the Smokey Mountains interfering with cell signals and transmitters, she, Benning and Olivia would be completely on their own.

Using the key she'd been given by Director Pembrook before leaving Knoxville, she pushed her way inside. Met with a spacious living room, pale stone and open ceilings, she dropped her duffel at her feet. The alarm panel to her right screamed for attention. She keyed in the code, also provided by the director, and moved to shed her coat. Pain registered as she pulled the heavy fabric from her shoulders, her T-shirt crusted to the wound. Securing the property—that was all that mattered right now. Then she could worry about digging the bullet from her side and recovering the evidence Benning had removed off that construction site. Heat brushed across her arms and neck as Benning carried his still-sedated daughter and her IV through the door. "You can put Olivia in one of the bedrooms over here. The fridge is fully stocked if you're hungry. I'll have someone on my team check in with her doctor about the head trauma protocol."

The girl had lost a lot of color in her face, her elvish features more gray now. Abducted, hospitalized, shot at. Ana could only imagine the nightmares coming when Olivia drifted off to sleep, and her heart lurched in her chest. To go through so much pain, at such a young age... It'd stay with her the rest of her life. Just as it'd stayed with Ana since she was that age.

But she had the chance to make sure that pain didn't tear Benning's family apart as it had her own.

"Thanks." He moved past her, the muscles along his neck and back flexing with every step as he headed around the short wall separating the entryway from the hallway. Smells of cinnamon and apples filled the space, but it would take a lot more than a few air fresheners to clear Benning's naturally intoxicating scent from her lungs. She'd been wrapped in a protective bubble with him for the past two hours inside the SUV. She wasn't sure if she could ever get him out from under her skin, but she'd keep her distance. His son's life depended on it.

Infierno. She forced herself to focus on the injury, peeling back the thin fabric of her T-shirt. To prove he didn't have this gripping hold over her. The bleeding had slowed, but the risk of infection out here was high. They were miles from any hospital, and with the bullet still inside, every move on her part only caused more damage. She had to secure the perimeter before arming the alarm system, then she could worry about the hole in her side. Sliding one arm back into her coat, she hissed as the pain increased.

"Where are you going?" That voice. His voice. Even after all these years, it hiked her pulse higher and heated her insides. How was that possible? She'd buried her feelings for him a long time ago. She'd moved on, healed. Four words out of his mouth shouldn't leave her wanting more.

"I need to make sure the security measures are up and running." A wide expanse of floor-to-ceiling windows revealed miles of wilderness, mountains and snow. If anyone had tracked them here, those trees would be the perfect cover, but safeguards had been put in place once the FBI had seized the cabin from its last owner. Cameras, motion-activated lights, heat sensors. All of it could've been compromised over the past few weeks of heavy snowfall. She'd check every single one of them before leaving Benning and Olivia on their own. They would be safe here, but the tension tightening the tendons between her neck and shoulders hadn't lessened. It was one thing to come back to Sevierville to find a missing boy. It was another to hole up in a safe house with a former fling for as long as it took to find that boy. More than that, she needed distance, needed to clear her head—of him. Dropping the magazine from her weapon, she counted her remaining rounds and slammed it back into place. She holstered her gun. "Shouldn't take too long. I'll brief my boss while I'm out. I should be able to get a team to the scene at your house in the next hour or so."

"Ana, wait." Her name whispered from his mouth, but she couldn't look up at him, couldn't allow him to see the battle she forged to keep her expression smooth. "I need you to understand something."

Six words. That was all it took for that small glimmer of hope she'd held on to to burn through her, but she couldn't afford to give it oxygen. It infiltrated the invisible barrier she'd built over the course of the past seven years, uninvited, and threatened to break through her control. Their relationship—however powerful it'd been—was over. She'd made sure of that when she'd transferred back to Washington, DC, without telling him.

"My kids are all I have, and I will do whatever it takes to protect them and to get my son back." One step. Two. He shortened the space between them until that hint of pine teased her senses again. "Even if that means throwing a wrench in the FBI's investigation."

What the hell did that mean?

"You requested me to work this case, Benning, to recover your son. That's exactly what I'm going to do, but if you want the person who took him to pay for what they've done, you're going to have to trust me." Turning toward the front door, she huddled inside her coat to head back out into the cold. Where she belonged, an outsider looking in. Not with Benning. Not with his daughter. This was just another case. Once upon a time, they'd talked about having a family of their own, but this one wasn't hers. They never would be. She'd meant every word during the drive out here. She'd dedicated her life and her career to finding the missing and that decision had ended their relationship. Attachment to each and every victim and their families was only a distraction to that cause. She'd learned that the hard way. Seven years ago she'd let those emotions get the best of her. She'd made a mistake, and a victim had paid the price. "You should get some rest. You and Olivia have been through a lot."

A wave of dizziness directed her shoulder into the nearest wall.

"You're not going anywhere." A strong hand threaded between her arm and the uninjured side of her rib cage and spun her into a hardened wall of muscle. She pressed against his chest, but Benning's massive body wouldn't budge. He'd put on more muscle over the years, the ridges and valleys fighting to escape his long-sleeve T-shirt. She imagined it'd partly been due to the fact he lived on the outskirts of town, on the property he'd inherited after his parents passed away. Calluses on his palms spoke of working the land with his bare hands. He was so much bigger than she was at over six feet; stronger, too, but he'd never used that strength to intimidate her. It wasn't part of his genetic makeup. He released his hold on her, giving her a chance to retreat, but she was paralyzed. Frozen in place with him so close. "You're bleeding through your coat."

"Comes with the territory of getting shot." Pain lightened through her nerve endings as though reminding her she had yet to pull the slug from her side. Right. With the rush of adrenaline from the shootout and every cell she owned tuned to every cell in his, her body's priority had been pushed to the back of her mind. Then again, she wouldn't be able to do her job if she bled out in the middle of the safe house.

He maneuvered her toward the dining room table. "You got a first-aid kit somewhere in this place?"

"Should be under the kitchen sink." She pulled one of the chairs away from the table and collapsed into the seat, hand clamped to her side. Sweat slid down her spine, her heart pounding at her temples. It'd been two hours since she'd been shot. Looked like her body had decided it wasn't going to be ignored any longer.

In seconds Benning returned with the red-and-white box, set the case on the table and settled into the chair beside hers. "Get rid of the shirt."

"I can stitch myself." She reached for the needle and thread inside the kit.

"I know you can, but you took that bullet for me

and Olivia." He took the supplies from her hand. "The least I can do is help get it out of you before you lose consciousness."

"Do you know what you're doing?" At this point she wasn't sure she cared.

"Owen needed stitches last year after running headfirst into that old fireplace on our property I should've knocked down years ago. My sewing skills seemed good enough for him." Cold worked across her skin as he cleaned away the excess blood with alcohol pads in efficient strokes.

"Do six-year-olds usually have strong opinions about head wounds?" she asked.

"He was more concerned about the fact the gash would leave a scar." Silence descended between them, every move made, every brush of his fingers against her skin, every breath he took, pinging on her radar. Loose strands of hair hid his face, but she didn't have to see him to know what was going through his head right now. She'd memorized his tells a long time ago. "Why did you come back here?"

"You don't remember? You requested me to work this investigation." She studied the deep lines set around his mouth. Not much had changed about him over the years. He was still handsome as ever, but there was a heaviness in the set of his eyes now. The same man she'd left behind sat mere inches away, but the past few years had left him weathered, battle torn. Rugged. He'd taken on the sole responsibility of raising his children and keeping his inspection business afloat. She couldn't imagine the amount of pressure that'd been thrust onto his shoulders practically overnight when he'd lost Lilly and ended up with two small newborns to care for alone. But the way he was looking at her now, the way her body responded to his touch... It was just the two of them. The investigation, their shared past, it all fled to the back of her mind. "Or did the man who broke into your house hit you harder than you thought?"

"You could've handed it off to one of the other agents on your team. The FBI has an entire division dedicated to this kind of thing." Benning discarded the bloodied wipes, then opened a fresh package and cleaned the oversize tweezers he'd set out a few minutes ago. Standing, he unbuckled his belt, bringing her attention to those powerful thighs wrapped in denim. "But you took this assignment anyway." He handed her his belt. "Here, bite down on this."

Ana clenched the leather between her teeth as he pried at the edges of the wound with the head of the tweezers. She forced herself to keep her body relaxed, but the pain got the best of her after a few seconds. Ana screamed against the fire scorching through her side as he fished the bullet out of her. In seconds Benning discarded the slug onto the kitchen table. She shut down the primal urge to lean just a bit closer, to touch him for some warped sense of comfort, and spit out the belt.

"Does it matter?" Deep down she knew the answer. Why she'd taken the case when she could've pushed it off onto another agent. It had nothing to do with redemption. "Finding victims is what I've been trained for, and I'm going to do whatever it takes to get your son back."

He nodded, threading the needle from the kit. After stitching the edges of her injury together in quick rows, he taped a fresh piece of gauze to her side and cleaned up the bloody mess she'd left behind. He stood over her. Bigger, more intimidating than he'd been a minute ago. "I know you will. Because if you can't, the bastard who took Owen is going to wish he'd killed me last night."

HE SMOOTHED THE backs of his knuckles across Olivia's forehead. The swelling where she'd hit her head—presumably when she'd jumped or been pushed from the kidnapper's SUV—had gone down, but she was still fighting against the sedatives the doctor had given her. Red flannel and pale bedding surrounded her small form on the queen-size bed. The saline bag attached to her IV had been emptied within the last hour, and he carefully unscrewed the connection, then wrapped her hand— needle and all—with gauze at the direction of her doctor's message. With only two beds in the massive cabin, he and Olivia would be bunking together, but he couldn't sleep. Not with Owen still out there. Alone. Afraid. His eyes burned as thoughts of how this investigation could end filled his head. If Benning handed over the skull he'd found in that building, what were the chances his son's kidnapper would let Owen go free? What would stop them from ripping Olivia's brother from her life?

"Can't sleep?" Her voice slid through him, stretching into the deepest parts of his mind to chase back the uncertainty clawing at him from inside. Ana's boots echoed off the hardwood floor as she closed the distance between her and the end of the bed. She'd gotten rid of the stained clothing, her shoulder holster and weapon stark against her white T-shirt, and in an instant, he had his answer. Ana. Ana would stop them from tearing his family apart. Just as she stopped so many others. She studied Olivia in the bed, then handed him a steaming mug of dark liquid.

"She's hogging the bed." The ceramic burned the oversensitized skin of his palms, but he only held the mug tighter. To keep him in the moment, to feel the pain. To remind himself that no matter how she still might affect his biological reactions, Ana was here to work this case and nothing more. He took a sip of his coffee. Decaf. "Unless you're willing to share?"

The idea drilled down through his core, eliciting too many tempting visuals.

"I think you felt me up enough getting the bullet out of my side." Her smile—the one he hadn't been able to forget after all these years—flashed wide, and his nerve endings caught fire. This right here. This was one of the reasons he'd fallen for her in the first place. The quick banter, her jokes. No matter how dark the situation, she'd always had the ability to lighten the mood, and the hollowness that'd carved straight through him the moment he'd learned she'd left him ebbed for the first time in years. Maneuvering around to his side of the bed, she pulled up a chair. The lamp beside his daughter's bed reflected the natural sheen of Ana's long, dark hair as she rested her heels on the edge of the mattress beside his. Would it still be as soft as he remembered? "I briefed TCD on the latest developments of the case. The director is sending two agents to your property to oversee processing the crime scene. Good agents, who know what they're doing. With any luck, they'll have something we can use to identify the man who took your son and where he's keeping Owen."

He didn't have to look at his wrist to see how many hours were left until the deadline the kidnappers had given him. It was as though the countdown clock had become part of his consciousness. Always there. Always ticking off the seconds one by one. Owen had been taken close to nine hours ago. The man who'd broken into his house had given him twenty-four to hand over the skull and any other evidence he'd uncovered before his son paid the price for his mistake. Would the agents sent by Tactical Crime Division be able to process the scene at his house before time ran out?

That all-too-familiar sense of instability rocked through him.

"I need to hand over the evidence." Benning shoved to his feet, his entire body buzzing with the need to take action. He should be out there looking for his son, doing whatever it took. Not holed up in some safe house imagining all the ways this investigation could go wrong. Placing the coffee mug on a side table, he scraped his fingernails across his scalp, shoulder-length hair caught between his fingers. Long stretches of trees and mountains on the other side of the massive floor-to-ceiling wall of windows increased the isolation growing inside. The sun had started dipping behind the Smokey Mountains. They were running out of time. Everything—the kidnapping, the shooting—it was all on him. "None of this would've happened if I hadn't started looking into Britland Construction. I should've left it alone. I'm the one who's supposed to be responsible for him. I promised him I would always keep him safe, and now Owen's out there in the hands of a possible killer because I wanted to play detective."

"You and I both know once you hand over that evidence, the person responsible for taking your son won't let you or your family walk away. You're too much of a risk." Her voice dipped to soothe the rough edges of anxiety tearing him apart from the inside. Movement registered from behind, and he turned to find her setting her own mug on the end table beside the bed. She closed the empty space between them without a single sound, taking special care not to wake Olivia. She motioned toward the bed with the crown of her head, but he couldn't look away from her, couldn't ignore the sudden shift in her expression. "Do you see that beautiful little girl there? She's alive because of you, Benning. You protected her from getting shot in that parking lot, and you tackled me to the floor in her room before the shooter could take me out. Neither of us would be here if it weren't for you."

She was right. Turning over the evidence wouldn't guarantee Owen's release, but his insecurity—the need for action—pricked at the back of his neck. "I want to be the one out there, looking for him."

"I know, and I know it doesn't feel like you're doing much, but I promise you, you are exactly where you need to be." Raising her hand, she settled it on his forearm. Heat and electricity coiled together in a dangerous combination that traveled down his spine. Tantalizing hints of her perfume nudged at the raw memories he'd tried to forget, and it took everything inside him not to give in. "We're going to get your son back. Together."

Her confidence, combined with her hand still on his arm, slowed his racing heart rate, and suddenly he was more aware of her than ever. Aware of the way her bangs settled along the curve of her cheeks, the way the swell of her lower lip was slightly fuller than the top and how the brown in her eyes had seemingly deepened over the past few minutes. She was a strong, intelligent, confident woman who'd committed herself to saving the lives of strangers on a daily basis, not to mention she was one of the most intense people he'd ever met. Admirable. Honest. Observant. Everything he thought he'd wanted in a life partner. Gravity pulled his gaze to her dark red fingertips resting against his skin. Until she'd left without a word. "Tell me why I had to find out you'd requested a transfer to Washington after you'd already left."

She let her hand slip away, the burn of her touch chased back by the cold penetrating through the wall of windows on his right. Diverting that mesmerizing gaze of hers toward his daughter in the bed, she took a step back. "Benning, we don't have to do this now."

"I was afraid you were dead." The admission tore from him. The hollowness he'd struggled to fill had been increasing every second since the moment she'd walked into that hospital room, and he couldn't take it anymore. "I called the police, the hospitals, the FBI, anyone who might've been able to tell me where you were or what'd happened to you. I looked for you for three days, Ana, with no phone calls, no messages, no emails or texts." He forced himself to take a deep breath before their conversation woke Olivia. "I woke up, and you were just…gone. I want to know—"

"Because my partner found her body." A hardness etched into her expression, her voice dropping into level territory. No emotion. No inflection. In an instant, the woman who'd joked with him a few minutes ago disappeared. Nothing but the cold, distant, detached federal agent he'd believed her capable of being all these years.

Confusion gripped him hard. "Whose body?"

"Samantha Perry," she said.

He'd heard that name before. Why did it sound so familiar? Somberness overcame him, his hands relaxing at his sides. Recognition flared as snippets of memory of his and Ana's first meeting rushed to the front of his mind. The first time he'd set eyes on her, she'd been partnered with another agent, but while Benning couldn't remember her partner's name, he could never forget Samantha Perry. Hell. "The teenage girl you'd come to Sevierville to find."

"They found her in the corner of an alley between two restaurants in Knoxville, discarded like a piece of trash three months after she disappeared." Her eyes remained steady on his, but almost absent, distant in the way she never blinked. "I was assigned to find her. I promised her family I would find her. She was an innocent fifteen-year-old girl who'd been taken from school by a janitor named Harold Wood who worked there, but we couldn't prove it. We searched his house, his car, the entire school. There was no sign of her, of her clothing, DNA, nothing, but her best friend swore she'd seen him on campus the day she went missing. The only proof that could've nailed that bastard to the wall was if her body turned up, but that wasn't good enough for me. I needed to find her alive, but I was too late. I failed her." Ana unfolded her arms, her gaze suddenly alive, the muscles across her shoulders hard. "She died because I let myself get distracted. With you."

His stomach dropped. A distraction?

"The minute I got that call from my partner, I swore to myself I would never let my emotions cloud my judgment again. So yes, I requested the transfer, and as soon as I got it, I left." She took a single step toward him. "Because every minute I wasn't focused on finding Samantha Perry was another minute she'd been tortured, violated and alone." Her expression smoothed as though she couldn't hold back the exhaustion and effects of blood loss anymore. Defeated. "I can't live with the weight of another life on my shoulders, Benning. Even for you."

Chapter Four

She strengthened her grip on the splintered wood railing off the cabin's back patio, staring out into nothing but darkness. Snowflakes clung to her hair and T-shirt as January temperatures dropped with the setting sun, but her heart rate hadn't slowed yet. Of all the people she'd been forced to discuss her part in that failed investigation with, she never thought Benning would be one of them. Then again, she never thought she'd have to come back here.

Her cover story hadn't been all that far off from the truth. Her parents were still living out their happily-ever-after, only not here. They'd relocated back west a few years ago for the warmer temperatures and open desert. As far as she knew, her three older brothers were still assigned to their respective law enforcement agencies, but it'd been years since she'd talked to or seen any of them, and right now she ached for that anchor. For something—someone—to keep her from getting dragged below the crushing weight she'd carried for the past seven years. Her family had tried to keep her head above water, but in the end, they'd realized there'd been nothing they could do to convince her Samantha Perry's death wasn't her fault. She'd have to live with that for the rest of her life.

It wasn't until Director Pembrook approached her in Washington a year ago—offered to give her a chance at redemption—that Ana had considered coming within one hundred miles of Sevierville. Because the truth was, leaving Benning had been one of the hardest decisions she'd ever had to make, even if it had been for the right reasons. Which didn't make sense. They'd only been seeing each other for a few months while she'd worked the Perry investigation, not nearly long enough to develop anything lasting. But she couldn't deny those short few months had changed everything.

The sliding glass door protested against the metal track from behind, but she didn't have the energy to face him yet. Forcing herself to take a deep breath, she studied the patterns her exhales made in front of her mouth. No matter what'd happened between them or how close to the surface her emotions seemed to get when he was near, she still had a job to do. Protect him and his family against the threat and get his son back. That was all that mattered. "You shouldn't be out here or anywhere close to the windows—"

"Are you a spy?" a small voice asked.

"What…" Ana turned to find Olivia huddled in one of the flannel blankets from her bed barefooted, a few feet away. Perfect ringlets of brunette hair framed round cheeks and bright blue eyes. Snow melted around the girl's purple-tipped toes, and she crouched low to level with the girl's gaze. She reached out, rubbing her hands up and down the girl's arms over the blanket to generate some semblance of heat, but with the light sheen of sweat clinging to the girl's face, Ana had a feeling the cold would have a hard time penetrating through. Curiosity bled into Olivia's wide-eyed expression. "What are you doing out here? You're going to freeze to death."

"Deflecting direct questions." The girl cocked her head to one side, suddenly seeming so much older than her six years of age. "That's exactly what a spy would do."

"I'm not a spy." Ana couldn't hold back the laugh escaping past her lips and reached into her back pocket for her credentials. Showing the girl her ID, she smiled as Olivia's small fingers smoothed over the plastic protector of her thin wallet. "I'm a federal agent. See?"

"Agent Ana Sofia Ramirez of the FBI." Olivia's smile stretched wide across her bruised face. "Cool! I've never met a federal agent before, but I read about them all the time. Detectives and private investigators, too."

"Yeah? Do you have a favorite?" Ana asked.

"There's a whole series about a girl Sherlock Holmes who solves crimes, but she's pretending to be a boy so the police don't know it's her." Animation chased back the dark circles from beneath Olivia's eyes, followed by pride. "I've read all the books six times."

"Wow. You must really like reading." Sliding her wallet back into the rear pocket of her jeans, Ana winced at the loud growls coming from her stomach. "You know what? I haven't eaten in a while, and I was thinking of making some chocolate chip cookies. How about I make the cookies, and you tell me about all the other books you've read?"

The girl nodded, then dragged her oversize flannel blanket edged with melted snow back into the cabin. Closing the sliding glass door behind them, Ana scanned the main floor, but didn't see any sign that Benning was aware his daughter had escaped her room. She wasn't a doctor. She didn't have the deciding power as to how long Olivia needed rest or if she should be out of bed at all. But Benning did, and the last thing she wanted was to step over the parenting line. Tensions between them were strung tight enough. "Do you think your dad would like some when we're done?"

"He's in the shower." Olivia climbed to the top of one of the bar stools at the counter's edge, the blanket falling from her small shoulders. Bruising darkened in thick patches across the girl's pale skin, the stitches across the laceration in her head somehow more pronounced now. It'd been ten hours since Olivia and her twin brother had been kidnapped.

Leaving only fourteen to get him back. "He doesn't know I'm awake, but I didn't want to sleep anymore."

"I see." After pulling the dry ingredients from the pantry, a few eggs and butter from the fridge, Ana set them out on the granite-topped island. Offering Olivia a whisk, she set about measuring the ingredients into a large bowl. "Well, I won't tell him you're out of bed when you're supposed to be resting if you don't tell him how much of this dough will actually be made into cookies. Deal?"

"Deal." Olivia took the whisk from her and attacked the ingredients as fast as she could. Flour, egg and sugar flew over the edges of the bowl onto the countertop, her laugh rising over the sounds of the metal whisk scraping against the bottom of the bowl.

"Okay. Take it slow. Slower." Ana automatically shot her hands out to save what was left of the batter. But after a few seconds nearly the entire contents of the bowl were spread across Olivia's stained pajamas, the countertop, and flecked into Ana's hair. Just witnessing the brightness in the girl's eyes after she'd had to suffer so much hurt lightened the persisting knot coiling tighter at the base of Ana's spine. In the next second the girl pulled the whisk up straight, big globs of unmixed ingredients dripping over as her smile flashed wide. Warning exploded through Ana's system. "No, no, no, no. I don't think so. Olivia, I swear, if you fling that at me, you're going to be in so much trouble—"

With a flick of Olivia's wrist, the batter flew straight across the island.

Gooey pieces of egg and dried blobs of batter slammed into Ana's face, then dropped down onto her clean shirt and the floor. *Santa madre de…* An exaggerated growl tore from her throat as she dashed through the kitchen to the other side of the counter. Feigned seriousness tainted her words. "I'm going to get you for that. I just changed into this shirt!"

Faster than she thought possible, Olivia jumped from the stool and ran to escape, the whisk still in her hand. Grabbing a spatula from the countertop, Ana scooped a chunk of cookie mix onto the utensil, then flung it across the kitchen. Olivia froze, her eyes and mouth wide. "Bull's-eye."

The next few minutes passed in a blur of flying cookie dough and laughs until both of them were too tired to move. Settling onto the floor, their backs against the island cabinets, Ana positioned the bowl of finished dough between them with two spoons. She fought to catch her breath. Over eight hundred hours of physically demanding firearms training and tactical operations, and she'd been worn out by a six-year-old with a penchant for mystery novels. Chunks of dough fell from cabinets across from them, but there would be plenty of time to clean up. Later. Right now they'd enjoy the sugar rush. The stitches in her side ached as her lungs struggled to keep up with her heart. "Whew. You, my friend, are a worthy opponent. I think you hit me way more times than I hit you."

Olivia scooped a spoonful of dough into her mouth. "I always win when me and Owen play Nerf guns. I'm a way better shooter than he is."

Ana set down her spoon. She'd been trained in child forensic interview techniques, the protocols running through her head. When it came to questioning children who'd been part of a crime or witnessed a crime, it was best to take it slow. She'd already developed a rapport with the girl, but there was a chance that not only wouldn't Olivia want to remember what'd happened to her brother but also couldn't because of the head trauma she'd sustained. Just as her doctors had diagnosed. "Can we talk about your brother? About what happened after that man took you away from your dad?"

The girl's chewing slowed, those bright blue eyes that matched her dad's losing a bit of light. Sliding her heels toward her rear, Olivia went back in for another scoop of dough, but something had changed. Could she have remembered something? Hesitation and nervousness played strong across her expression. Her heart-shaped lips rolled between her teeth. "I don't remember anything."

"Okay." But it certainly looked like Olivia was keeping something to herself. "But you know not even your favorite Sherlock Holmes can solve a case unless she has all the information she needs. I would really like to find your brother for you, Olivia. For you and your dad. Isn't that what you want?"

"No!" The girl shoved to her feet, throwing the spoon as hard as she could across the kitchen. Those ringlet curls bounced off her shoulders as she dashed across the house.

"Olivia, wait!" Ana ran after her.

"Olivia, what are you doing out of bed?" Benning's soothing voice preceded the rest of him. His damp, glistening bare chest reflected the droplets of water dripping from his shoulder-length hair. He lowered into a crouch to catch his daughter around the waist, dressed in nothing but a pair of jeans, and Ana's heart threatened to beat out of her chest. Familiar blue eyes, immediately darker in that instant, locked on her. "What's wrong? What happened?"

Sobs racked through Olivia's body as the girl buried her head between Benning's neck and shoulder, and Ana could do nothing but watch. Every moment of the fun she and Olivia had had together vanished in the span of a few words. "I don't want to remember!"

BENNING CLOSED THE door to his and Olivia's room behind him. He'd calmed her down enough to quiet her sobs, but nothing would settle the fear hooking deep into her head. She didn't want to remember what'd happened when she and her brother had been taken, and he couldn't blame her. There was nothing he could do—nothing he could say—to make

his six-year-old daughter believe she wasn't responsible for what'd happened to Owen, even if she had
been able to remember something that would help
find him. And he wasn't about to push her fragile
mental state more than he already had. Abducted,
suffering head trauma, being shot at... Olivia had
been through more in the past ten hours than most
children experienced in their entire lives. How much
more could he honestly expect her to take before
she broke?

Fisting the T-shirt he'd discarded before hitting
the shower, he headed back toward the kitchen bare-
foot. Even with the self-imposed distance between
them and the outburst from his daughter, he couldn't
get Ana's words out of his head. She blamed herself
for the death of that girl, the teenager who'd gone
missing seven years ago. But deeper than that, she
blamed him. Isn't that what she'd meant when she'd
sworn not to let her emotions cloud her judgment
again? That the feelings they'd had for each other
had caused her to lose focus? It'd taken both of them
jumping into that relationship with both feet, and
that made him as much responsible for her imagined failure. He and Ana had only been together for
a few months, but those few months had been the
most intense days of his entire life. He remembered
every second of them, and the fact that Ana was
trying to forget—to discount everything between
them—knotted his gut tighter.

Every cell in his body froze as he stepped directly

in a wet pile of what he hoped to hell was raw cookie dough. The island in the center of the kitchen was a mess. Flour, egg shells, sugar and random land mines of chocolate chips scattered over the countertop. Bowls, whisks, measuring cups. The place resembled a battlefield, and there, in the center of it all, Ana attempted to clear the casualties from the cabinets. He couldn't help but smile at the combination of small bare footprints and larger boot prints dusted into the floor. "Did you at least win?"

"Not even close. But to the loser go the spoils." Turning, she pushed her bangs out of her face. She held up a half-eaten bowl of unbaked dough, specs of flour and butter crusted into her hair, as she spooned a mouthful of sugar and butter past her lips. His heart jerked in his chest. In that moment she wasn't the federal agent assigned to recover his son. Right then, she was the woman who'd gotten his daughter to laugh. That sound, the sound of Olivia's exaggerated screams, had pulled him from the shower, but what he'd seen would be burned into his memories forever. Ana chasing his daughter around the counter with a spatula. Olivia's wide smile that he feared he'd never see again after what she'd witnessed. For those gut-wrenching seconds, the kidnapping, the evidence he'd stashed on his property, the reason for Ana coming back into his life… It'd all disappeared. In a matter of minutes he'd gotten a real-life glimpse into the fantasy he'd constructed in his head. A family—his family—complete. Happy.

"That right there makes losing worth it. I'd offer to share, but I don't want to." Speaking around her mouthful of dough, she studied the stains across her shirt, the dish towel still in one hand, and Benning couldn't help but follow her gaze across the long, lean muscle running the length of her body. Heat speared through him as the past rushed to meet the present. The feel of her skin against his, how he'd memorized every scar, every mole, with his hands. She hadn't changed a whole lot over the course of the few years. If anything, Ana Sofia Ramirez had only become more beautiful, more…tempting. "Although, I'll admit I didn't think she'd destroy me this bad."

"You got hustled." He hobbled to the kitchen sink to clean the dough off his foot. Trying to focus on the raw egg stuck under his heel instead of the re-action his study of her had ripped through him, he gave in to the laugh rumbling in his chest. "That girl asked me to teach her how to shoot my rifle when she was four years old so she could help the police solve crimes. The only way I can ever get her to calm down during a temper tantrum is to promise to let her listen to an episode of a true crime podcast. She loves the idea of saving lives and catching bad guys and has better aim than anyone else I know. She's not afraid to show it, either. Next, she'll want me to take her to the police station to ask if she can help solve one of their cases."

"Well, maybe I can give her a tour of TCD head-quarters in Knoxville one day. You know, give her a chance to see what federal agents really do on the job." Ana stilled, the weight of her attention pressurizing the air in his chest, but he didn't miss the assumption there would be a *one day* for them. That she wouldn't disappear from their lives after Owen came home, and his blood pressure spiked. She cleared her throat as though she'd caught herself making promises she might not be able to keep. Just as she had with Samantha Perry's family. "You must be proud. She's going to make a hell of an agent one day."

"That's her plan, and probably why she opened up to you the way she did. I can tell she admires you, what you do." Benning straightened, echoes of their earlier conversation replaying in his head on a nonstop loop. He tossed the paper towel he'd used to clean his foot in the trash beside the island. "So do I, to be honest. The work you and your team do saves lives. I know I already said thank you, but I meant it."

"Like I said, you don't have to thank me." She dropped that mesmerizing gaze to the counter, sweeping the spread of flour into the sink set into the island with one hand, and swiped beneath her nose with the other. Touching her face had always been a nervous habit. "All part of the job."

"Is that what this is for you, Ana? Just another job? Because this case is definitely a lot more personal to me." Benning maneuvered around the counter, his bare chest nearly pressed against the exposed skin of her arm. He set his hand over hers on the granite, her quick gasp searing through him. Her warmth penetrated past skin and muscle, deep into his bones. "After what you told me about the Samantha Perry case, I realize now how hard it must've been for you to come back here, and you're standing there as if none of it affects you. But is that how you really feel?"

He wanted—no, *needed*—to know. Was this going to play out exactly as it had between them the last time? Had he made a mistake requesting her to work this case?

Her mouth parted. "I…"

Skimming his fingers along the back of her hand, he trailed a path up her arm to her jaw, and all of his thoughts burned away. There was only the two of them. The softness of her flawless skin and hardness in her invisible guard. After everything that'd happened, after everything they'd already been through in the short span of time she'd walked back into his life, he'd struggled to keep the uncertainty, the rage, the fear, at bay so he could stay strong for Olivia. To prove that he could protect her from any threat, be the father she and her brother deserved. But Ana… stripped him of all of that. With her, Benning felt raw, exposed, bare. She was real. She was here. Not a memory—a fantasy—anymore, and it took everything inside him to pull himself away from her. "You had some cookie dough on your chin."

She'd left because she believed her emotions clouded her judgment on the Samantha Perry case, and he wasn't about to complicate anything else between them. Not when it was his son's life at risk this time. Ana turned her gaze up to his, a small tremor crossing her shoulders, and an invisible anchor settled inside his chest in the dark, watery landscape of this case. No matter what happened, Ana would bring his son home alive. He had to believe that. He had to believe in her. Otherwise, he'd have nothing left. "Thanks."

A soft trill broke the silence spreading between them, but she didn't move.

"I think your phone is ringing." He cleared his throat, trying to drown the surge of awareness burning through him, and stepped away. It was for the best. Because anything that happened between them would only take away from their focus on finding his son, and that wasn't a risk he was willing to take.

Ana pulled her phone from her back pocket, running one hand through her hair, but only ended up streaking more flour into the soft strands. Tapping her cell's screen, she answered the call and pressed Speaker. "What do you have for me, JC?"

The agent she'd called from the car. The muscles down Benning's spine contracted as every sense he owned homed in on the voice on the other end of the line. Had the team dispatched to the crime scene at his house found something that could tell them where Owen was being held? He hiked his T-shirt over his head and shoved his arms through.

"Sevierville PD is still working the scene, but I can tell you right now, it's not looking good," JC said.

Tension replaced the rush of sudden desire through-out Benning's body. What the hell did that mean? Static cut through the line, but given the cabin's proximity to the Smokeys, it was a miracle they'd received the call at all. They were two hours out of town, with nothing and no one around but trees, the mountains and wildlife.

Three distinct lines deepened between Ana's dark eyebrows. "What are you talking about?"

"We searched the property and found the old out-door fireplace a few hundred feet from the house you'd told us about. Kinda hard to miss seeing as how the entire thing was on fire. Bad news is, that skull you sent the photo of with the gunshot wound wasn't inside," JC said.

"How is that possible?" Benning didn't under-stand. "No one knew that's where I hid it."

"That's not all," JC said. "We might not have the skull you wanted, but the coroner did pull an entire set of bones from the fireplace once we got the fire under control, and, Ana, the remains… It's going to be nearly impossible to identify them now."

THE BASTARD HAD used an accelerant.

The odor of gasoline burned Agent JC Cantrell's nostrils, even with his nose and mouth buried in the crease of his elbow. Crime scene techs and the cor-oner carefully removed the charred remains one by one from the brick fireplace hidden back on Benning Reeves's property as he disconnected his call with Ramirez.

Hell, the only reason they'd found the fireplace had been because the whole damn thing had been on fire, which meant their UNSUB—unidentified suspect—hadn't just taken Benning Reeves's kids last night, he'd also come back to clean up his own mess. Assuming it was the same perp behind both crimes. Black smoke still lingered in the air and irritated his eyes. It was a miracle the flames hadn't started a wildfire, but whoever'd lit the match most likely hadn't even thought about the possibility. They'd been too busy trying to cover up a crime by destroying evidence. Which, from the looks of the blackened bones currently being sealed into evidence bags, had done a damn fine job.

He followed the pattern of scorch marks scarred into the dim red bricks. Gasoline burned upward of five hundred degrees, but add in the fact those bricks held on to that heat and the metal inside the fireplace, there was a good chance dental records, fingerprints and DNA had all been burned away. Without an ID on the body, the chances of that six-year-old boy coming home only got smaller. "Damn it."

Sevierville PD had taped off the target scene with a wide perimeter through the trees at JC's instruction, the entire property in controlled chaos. Local PD had already searched and processed the house, but out here it'd take days—weeks—to filter through what qualified as evidence. Small towns like this saw a few instances of violent crime, but this case was about to blow Sevierville's crime stats through the roof. Someone had used the fireplace out of convenience, knowing the remains would be found, but they hadn't wanted the victim to be identified. That was where the accelerant came in. With any luck and depending on how long the fire had been going, the forensic lab might still be able to put a rush on pulling DNA from the bone marrow of the victim and nail this killer to the wall. JC would be there when they did.

He noted the shortened bones of the hand the coroner was in the process of securing. He faced Evan Duran, hostage negotiator extraordinaire, crouched a few feet away, and dropped his arm away from his mouth and nose. "Looks like our UNSUB went out of his way to ensure pulling fingerprints were out of the question. Cut the tips of the victim's fingers clean off before lighting the match."

"The guy knows what he's doing, that's for sure. That's why we couldn't trace the bug he planted in Olivia Reeves's hospital room and couldn't get any surveillance of the getaway vehicle the night of the kidnapping. I'd say our suspect has at least some knowledge of crime scenes or forensics given he chose to toss in the gasoline." Duran straightened, gaze to the ground as he moved farther from the epicenter of the crime scene. This case had the entire Tactical Crime Division team on edge. Hell, JC couldn't even imagine what was going through

Ramirez's head right now having to partner with a former lover to find the guy's son, but for Duran, this investigation hit a little too close to home. The hostage negotiator's little sister had been taken from right in front of their apartment building when he was only ten years old, too small to do anything but watch, but it was that moment that drove Duran's attention to this case now. He would do whatever it took to bring Owen Reeves home. They all would. Shadows darkened Duran's Latino features as he nodded to the trail carved through the mud. "But he wasn't careful enough."

"What do you got?" JC arced his path out from his teammate's to avoid contaminating whatever Duran had found. Slowing, he caught sight of the deep grooves carved into the snow and mud—most likely drag marks from his victim's heels—coming from the house and snapped a pair of latex gloves over his hands. Cold worked past the thick layer of his coat the longer they searched the scene, but the sight of a silver or white gold piece of jewelry partially uncovered in the dirt froze him straight through. A charm in the shape of the scales of justice with the eyelet spread wide as though it'd been torn from a necklace or bracelet. He swiped up on his phone's screen and took a photo before digging for an evidence bag from his jacket. He pinched the metal between his index finger and thumb and dropped it inside.

"Might help us identify the victim," Duran said.

"The coroner would've mentioned if there'd been

evidence of jewelry melted to the bones. Gasoline burns hot, but not hot enough to evaporate silver or white gold." JC pushed to his feet, studying the charm still in his hand. Sunlight pierced through the trees, reflected off the tarnished metal. His lungs still burned with the smell of gasoline and dropping temperatures. They were losing daylight. In another hour Sevierville PD would have to pull out the spotlights, making it that much harder to search the scene. "Which means it came from somewhere else."

From someone else. Another victim? Were they about to find more bodies out here? JC messaged the photo he'd taken directly to Ramirez. Scanning the trees around them, he couldn't shake the feeling every piece of evidence they recovered, every move they'd made out here, was being carefully curated and watched. The vibration of his phone snapped him back into reality, and he answered Ramirez's call. "You get the picture I sent?"

"Where did you get that charm?" A combination of tension and panic tinted her words, and everything around JC slowed. Ramirez wasn't the kind of agent to wear her emotions on her sleeve, but something about this charm had obviously rattled her.

"You recognize it." Not a question. He leveled his gaze with Duran's, the hairs on the back of his neck standing on end.

One second. Two.

"Ramirez?" JC checked the screen. The call hadn't been dropped.

"Yes. I recognize it. It belonged to a fifteen-year-old girl whose body was found a few months after she went missing from Sevierville. Her name was Samantha Perry," Ramirez said. "I was one of the agents assigned to find her."

Chapter Five

It wasn't possible. Samantha Perry's charm shouldn't have been at that crime scene. Not unless... The edge of her phone cut into her hand, her gaze rising to meet Benning's. "Search the rest of the property. I need you to find that skull and get me an ID on the victim. Now," she ordered JC.

She disconnected the call, the entire floor shaking beneath her as though a high-magnitude earthquake had rolled through Sevierville. Or maybe the possibility of a familiar killer had her senses on the edge of an unknown precipice. She didn't know. Didn't care. The FBI had been hunting Samantha's murderer for seven years with no leads, no evidence, no crime scene left behind. Nothing. Until now. Couldn't be a coincidence. She fought to control her breathing, an acidic bite on her tongue, but gravity had drained the blood from her upper body too fast.

"Ana?" Her name on his lips, that seductive combination of a growl and concern, pushed at the barriers she'd set between her and the rest of the world. "Tell me what happened."

"Have you seen this charm before? Could it be Olivia's or one of her friends'?" Swiping her tongue across her dry lips, she angled her phone toward him, the screen bright with the photo JC had sent.

"No. The only piece of jewelry Olivia has is a beaded necklace she made herself." He shook his head. "I don't let her or the kids' friends go that deep into the woods. Not after Owen cut open his head on that fireplace."

"Agents Cantrell and Duran found this bracelet charm near the crime scene on your property after the coroner pulled an entire set of remains from that same fireplace. The girl who went missing when we were… Samantha Perry." No. Now wasn't the time to fall back into the past, no matter how much she wanted to sink into the familiar cage of his body around hers. There were too many similarities between then and now, but she couldn't afford to let the past dictate the present. "She had one exactly like it. She and her best friend had a matching set. Only Samantha's wasn't recovered with her body. They found her bracelet, but the charm had been torn off."

He took the phone from her, his calluses catching on the side of her hand, but where her body had instantly warmed at their brief contact mere minutes ago, the hollowness inside only tore through her now. "Justice scales?"

"It's the zodiac sign for Libras. Both girls shared

the same birthday. They were friendship charms."
What were the chances another charm like that
would surface now, right when Ana had come back
to Sevierville? "My partner and I theorized Samantha's killer kept it as a trophy, but we couldn't prove
it. Harold Wood disappeared off the FBI's radar. He
quit his job at the school, wasn't seen by any of his
neighbors or his family in the area. No one has been
able to find him for seven years."

"But now the charm's surfaced, and someone
burned a body on my property." He handed her back
the phone, but the numbness spreading through her
was all consuming as he stumbled backward. Color
drained from his face, his wet hair leaving pools of
dampness across his shoulders. "You think the man
who killed Samantha Perry has something to do with
Owen's kidnapping?" He ran his hands through his
hair, fisting the dark strands. "What about the victim they found? Was it… Could it be—"

"No." She rushed toward him, her hands gripped
around his muscled arms to keep him upright. *Infierno.* His skin was hot. She battled against the
possibility of his six-year-old boy being held by a
vicious killer, but she couldn't discount anything
at this point. That charm had been discovered on
Benning's property, mere feet from a fireplace that
contained human remains. The chances that specific
piece of jewelry had turned up in not one but two
of her investigations were slim, but the idea Owen
Reeves had been taken by the same monster who'd

killed Samantha Perry... Nausea churned in her gut. She sought his gaze and put every ounce of confidence she had left into her voice. "It wasn't your son, Benning. Agent Cantrell said the remains belong to an adult. Owen is still out there. He still needs our help."

"Someone took the skull and stuffed another body in there?" Mountainous shoulders rose and fell in rapid succession as he leveled bright blue eyes with hers. "You said you needed an ID on the victim they found right away. You already have an idea of who the victim is."

She nodded. After all these years, how could he still read her so easily? How could one look from him make her forget why she'd left in the first place? She swallowed hard against the urge to lean a bit closer, to confirm the unsettling pressure inside was nothing more than biology in a stress-induced situation and had nothing to do with the man standing in front of her. Ana forced her fingers to unwrap from around his arms, the heat sliding past her defenses too familiar, too comforting. Too tempting. "You said your nanny should've been there with the kids when you got back home. The killer might've gotten to her first and taken advantage of the fireplace to get rid of her body. Or... Samantha's best friend owned the same charm bracelet. She would be an adult now, but if it doesn't belong to Samantha, then, given the fact her best friend is the one who led us to him as a suspect, there's a possibility he resurfaced here in Sevierville for another victim. For Claire. Either way, there's a chance whoever took your son has the skull, too."

The rush of his exhale swept across her neck and collarbones. "You make it sound like this guy is a serial killer."

"Somebody drywalled that skull into one of Britland's construction projects, used your kids as leverage because you found it, and is now trying to tie up loose ends by destroying the evidence." In her experience, that didn't sound like the plan of a serial killer. Not with the seven-year cooling-off period and differences in MO between the victims. But Ana couldn't ignore the number of victims missing in this investigation or the charm found on Benning's property. No. The random—almost chaotic—moves this killer had made spoke of something much more dangerous. "I think whoever we're dealing with is desperate to hide what they've done. No matter who gets in their way."

"Just tell me what I need to do to get my son back," Benning said.

"We start where this all began. Finding the skull. If we can pinpoint how and why the victim ended up in that wall, we'll find who put them there." Her phone vibrated from another incoming message from JC. Crime scene photos. She scanned through the shots her teammate had taken of the remains as the coroner sealed each bone into individual evidence bags. How the rest of the bones had gotten there, she didn't know. She had to assume whoever'd started the fire had tried to destroy the evidence all at once. She wanted to be there, wanted a firsthand look at the scene, wanted to do something that would help the investigation and not make it so she didn't feel so…helpless, but as long as Benning and his daughter were in danger, Ana would stay. She'd do for them what she hadn't been able to for Samantha Perry. She'd protect them.

She studied the photos. The fire had most likely burned away any chance of comparing DNA from the remains, so it'd be almost impossible to identify the victim, but the slight discoloration on a few of the skull's fragments—different than the rest—held her attention. Evidence of blunt-force trauma. The photo Benning had taken of the skull he'd recovered flashed across her mind. The owner of the skull from the construction site had been shot in the head. Not hit from behind. Another difference in MO. "The skull you found. What did it look like when you pulled it out of the wall?"

He moved to her side. "You mean aside from the fact it wasn't attached to the rest of the body?"

"I mean was there evidence of blood, mold?" She wasn't trained in forensics, but even the smallest clue might help them date how long the remains had been sealed behind the drywall or where the victim had died. "Was there a distinct odor?"

"Actually, it seemed like it'd been there for a while." He rubbed his hand across the back of his neck. "The building I found it in is one of Britland

Construction's oldest ongoing projects. I found out construction has been on hold for almost five years because of all the settlements the company is dealing with."

"So it could've been sealed behind the wall anywhere from a few months to years." Decaying bodies emitted gases as bacteria broke down cells over time. Whoever'd hidden the remains had to have used something to cover up the odor. They'd had access to that building and hadn't expected anyone to find that head for years, if ever, but then Benning had started investigating Britland. He'd put a target on his back by getting too close to the truth, and the killer had known the moment he'd removed the remains and lashed out to keep their secret. But none of that explained the possible connection to the Samantha Perry case.

"I'll start by looking into employment records for Britland and run background checks on their personnel. If this is tied to them, that should give us what we need so I can narrow our suspect list down to the man who took your son." And find out how that charm had ended up at the crime scene on Benning's property. She tucked her chin to her chest as awareness of how close he'd gotten rocketed through her. Stepping away, she pocketed her phone, her insides cooling instantly with his lack of body heat adding to hers. She fisted the dish towel she'd been using to clean up after her and Olivia's cookie dough fight in an attempt to lock down her body's visceral reaction, and tossed it into the kitchen sink with the dishes. In vain.

In the short few hours she'd been back in Sevierville, the time that'd kept them apart, the distance she'd wedged between them, the complete and utter focus on her cases... It'd all faded. As much as she hated the idea he could still affect her after all this time—after everything she'd worked to bury—that deep, lingering attraction held tighter than ever before. But she couldn't risk giving it more power over her than she already had. Not when it jeopardized her ability to do her job. "With any luck, the medical examiner will have an ID and cause of death on the victim from the fireplace in the next couple of hours, and we can connect the two to get your son back."

She headed for the duffel she'd dropped at the front door with her laptop inside. Running through Britland employment records. Identifying the victim who'd been burned in the fireplace on Benning's property. Finding his son. Nothing else mattered. They'd already wasted so much time. She didn't dare give in to any more distractions.

"Ana, wait." Callused fingers slipped around her arm, swinging her into a wall of muscle. He didn't move, her exhales mingling with his. Her brain locked on to the fact his free hand had drifted to her waist, and she couldn't think beyond the searing heat seeping past her skin. "I just..." Hesitation lightened his hold on her as a darker shift deepened the color of his eyes.

Then he crushed his mouth to hers.

HER SPINE OF steel hardened under his touch, triggering every cell in his body into mind-numbing protest. But instead of pulling away, the woman who'd walked out on him years before sighed against his mouth. That sound, so small, so vulnerable despite her toughened exterior, only added fuel to the raging desire burning through his veins. She was everything he remembered and more. Soft but strong, unapologetic and honest, confident yet afraid of failure. Ana was the kind of woman if threatened with battle, she brought an entire war, a warrior who never backed down and never gave up. And there wasn't a damn thing he'd been able to do over the years to get her out of his head, no matter how many times he'd tried. Now, with her here, fighting to save his family, he wasn't sure it was possible. Or if he wanted it to be.

He penetrated the seam of her lips, memorizing her all over again as she arched against him. Her fingernails scraped against his scalp as she threaded her hand through his hair, and in an instant he was lost. In her. In the way her heart beat hard at the base of her throat, in her light sultry scent, in the way she'd managed to make him forget years of uncertainty and isolation with a single smile. Lean muscle flexed and released as he explored the smooth skin along her back. Things had changed between them. They'd gone their separate ways in an attempt to move on, to forget what'd happened between them, but this—the feel of her skin against his, the taste of her in his mouth—he'd missed this. Missed her. He'd given everything he could to make his marriage to Lilly work, loved his children more than he'd imagined possible, but the damage Ana had carved through him when she'd abandoned him had only torn deeper over time. Had left him hollow. Until now. "Ana—"

"We…" She pressed her hand against his chest, directly over his pounding heart. Hazel-green eyes lifted to his as she swiped something from his bottom lip with the pad of her thumb, sensation spreading across his face and down his neck. One word. That was all it took to bring him back to reality, to remind him of what was at stake if they took this any further, to remind him that there were lives at risk. His son's life was at risk. She sank back onto the four corners of her feet and increased the empty space between them. She pressed the back of her hand against her mouth, a combination of regret and horror contorting her smooth expression that pierced straight through him. Shaking her head, Ana dropped her gaze to the floor. "We can't do this, Benning."

"I know." Dread pooled at the base of his spine. She was right. They couldn't do this. Because of the case. Because she blamed herself—her feelings for him—as the cause for that girl's death, and he didn't know what the hell had come over him other than he hadn't been able to keep his distance from her for even another fraction of a second.

For years he'd kept himself in check. He'd buried his feelings for her at the back of his mind and tried to forget the rookie FBI agent who'd turned his entire world upside down. He'd thrown himself into taking care of his kids and building his company, but the moment he'd caught sight of her running around the kitchen island, chasing after his daughter with a spatula full of raw cookie dough, he'd realized it'd all been for nothing. Every minute they'd been together for those short few months had left an undeniable mark.

All this time he'd been turning down dates, offers of coffee, or grabbing lunch in the name of protecting his kids from losing yet another feminine influence in their lives. Protecting himself from getting too attached—from getting hurt—but when it came right down to it, he'd been holding out for her to come back into his life. Now here she was, more out of reach than ever before, and all he could do was laugh. "You're right, and I'm sorry. You've made it perfectly clear you don't have feelings for me."

"You say that like I didn't feel anything for you when we were together," she said.

He pulled his shoulders back. "Did you? Because you certainly made walking away in the middle of the night look easy."

Her fingers curled into fists at her sides, as though she was preparing for battle, and hell if he wasn't ready for it. Shadows smoothed the emotions from her features, every detail of her face guarded in an instant. "My job is saving lives, Benning. I'm trying to bring as many victims home to their families as I can, and letting what happened between us distract me from finding your son only makes it harder—"

"Damn it, love isn't a distraction, Ana." He hadn't meant his admission to roar past his defenses, but there it was. Out in the open. His heart threatened to beat straight out of his chest, lungs fighting to catch up with his fight-or-flight response. He understood the importance of her work, why she'd dedicated her life to bringing home the missing, why her brothers had all chosen law-enforcement careers, and he needed that cause now more than ever. But there had to be a point where she couldn't blame herself for the actions of the monsters she chased. She deserved more than taking on one assignment after the next with nothing to gain. Didn't she realize that? All she had to do was face that truth. Her little sister, Samantha Perry, all of the victims she hadn't been able to find over the years? They weren't coming home, and closing herself off from feeling that loss—or much of anything else—would only destroy her from the inside.

"Love?" The single word struggled past her kiss-stung lips. Her gaze connected with his. "Benning, I wasn't… We didn't—"

"I was in love with you." He shortened the distance she'd wedged between them as the sun disappeared behind the ridge of the Smokeys through the windows. Worn wood flooring protested under his weight, the only break in silence settling throughout the cabin. Benning locked his jaw against the urge to touch her, straightening as he lowered his voice. "Listen, I know why you're out there saving lives. I know why you push yourself so hard and why you've detached yourself from connecting with the people around you. But now it's my son who's been taken, and I need you to care. I need the woman I fell in love with seven years ago working this case because she's my only chance of getting him back. Not the empty shell she's trying to become."

He didn't wait for her response. Turning on his heels, he headed for the cabin's front door and didn't stop until he'd disarmed the alarm and stepped into the biting cold. Silent flakes fell around him as he stared out into the trees from the front porch. He could still taste her on his mouth, the slight hint of chocolate mixed with sugar and butter from the cookie dough on the back of his tongue. What the hell had he been thinking, kissing her while his son was out there in the hands of his abductor? That was the problem when it came to Ana. He couldn't think. Couldn't remember to breathe. Logic and self-preservation didn't exist when he got close to her, but knowing now that she hadn't felt the same way toward him as he had for her, that cleared up a lot of confusion. Back then he'd wanted, he'd taken, and he hadn't given a damn about the consequences. Only now he had Owen and Olivia to think about, and his son would be the only one to pay the price if he let himself slip again.

He forced one foot in front of the other down the steps. Benning kicked through the six inches or so of snow toward the remains of a tree stump and pile of firewood along the side of the cabin. Wrapping his stiffening fingers around the handle of an ax embedded in the stump, he pulled the blade free. Muscle memory kicked in as he used the weight of the ax head to slide his hand lower on the handle and centered a log upright on the stump. Calluses from the thousands of times he'd chopped wood on his own property frictioned against the wooden handle. He'd lived his entire life in Sevierville, taken over his father's inspection business and worked the twenty acres of land he'd inherited from his parents with his own two hands. No matter what'd come his way, he'd found a way to keep his family's heads above water and food on the table, but he couldn't fix this. Couldn't make Ana feel something she didn't want to feel.

"Seven years." He rotated his shoulder as he swung the ax blade back and around. The crack of wood filled his ears as the log split down the middle and fell to either side of the stump. The breath he'd been holding rushed out of him, instantly freezing just beyond his mouth. The sun had gone down, the cabin's motion-detecting lights washing over him and the snow around him, but the weight of being watched never surfaced. Ana had most likely gone to do exactly what she'd said she would. Run background checks on Britland Construction employees and shut out everything that didn't matter to the investigation. Including him. Sweat built at the base of his spine as he swung again. And again. Exhaustion, exertion, guilt. Fatigue worked through his muscles after a dozen swings, but he wouldn't stop. Not until he got his head back on straight. Although one thing was certain now: as soon as he and Ana brought his son home—ended this nightmare—he'd be the one to walk away.

Yet, for a brief moment she'd kissed him back.

A twig snapped somewhere beyond the tree line to his right, and Benning slowed the ax's next arc. The blade swept across his pant leg as he scanned the darkness ahead for the source. Out here, this far up against the mountains, outlined black bear territory. He tightened his hold on the ax between both hands as the hairs on the back of his neck stood on end. Taking a step back, he listened for any other sign of movement.

Then pain exploded across his head from behind, and the world went black.

Chapter Six

Her middle finger hung poised above her laptop keyboard as she forced herself to read, for the third or fourth time, each and every Britland Construction employee name TCD had forwarded on, but none of the names registered. She couldn't focus. Couldn't ignore the bright warning of motion-sensor detection from the south side of the cabin on the right side of her screen. Benning had stormed out so fast, she hadn't gotten the chance to disarm the sensors, but from the soft rhythmic thumping coming from outside, she imagined he'd found the firewood and ax.

She'd confirmed his retelling of events with a digital copy of the Sevierville police report filed last night. Site security had called police after shots had been fired by an unknown shooter in a black ski mask, who'd escaped before officers arrived, but they hadn't gotten a clear look at the man who'd been on the other end of the barrel before he'd run. Benning.

I need the woman I fell in love with... Not the empty shell she's trying to become.

He'd fallen in love with her. Ana gripped the edges of the countertop until her knuckles whitened against the translucent skin there. Hints of dropping temperatures bled through the windows, but it was the cold sliding through her insides that kept her cemented in place. Benning had fallen in love with her seven years ago, but he didn't think she was capable of feeling anything for him. Didn't think she cared about the little boy he'd asked her to find. Isn't that what he'd said? That she'd made disappearing in the middle of the night look easy. Because she was just an empty shell.

The kitchen lights flickered above, then died. Ana raised her gaze to the ceiling, her attention sliding down the walls toward the front door. The familiar LED light on the alarm panel on the wall blinked rapidly. The cabin's previous owner had programmed a backup generator to automatically kick on when the property lost power, a necessity considering how far they were from civilization. But after a full minute, the lights remained dark.

And the thumping from outside had stopped. "Benning?"

Warning skittered up her spine, raising a trail of goose bumps across her shoulders. Ana unholstered her weapon but kept it at her side as she stepped into the main living space. She heel-toed it slowly toward Olivia's bedroom, old wood groaning beneath her feet. No movement through the windows. Nothing but the sound of her own breathing. Routine blackouts occurred frequently throughout the area, but that didn't explain why the generator hadn't started. She'd checked the fuel levels and connections during her initial perimeter search. The tank had been full. Which meant it had to have been disconnected.

Wrapping her hand around the bedroom doorknob, she shouldered her way inside Olivia's room. Curtains drawn, lights out. It took a few seconds for her eyes to adjust, but the soft outline of Olivia beneath the covers—asleep—brought her racing heart rate down a notch. Ana reached her free hand around the door and twisted the lock before closing it behind her. No matter what happened, nothing would get through this door. She'd make sure of it.

She skimmed her fingers across the alarm panel beside the front door and hit the panic button. No response. Her stomach sank, and she raised her weapon parallel with the floor. Whoever'd cut the power and the generator must've also cut the lines to outside contact. Unpocketing her cell phone, she checked for coverage. Nothing reliable. *"Maldicion."*

As of right now she was all that stood between the threat and Benning and his daughter. She shoved her phone back into her pocket. After dropping the magazine from her service weapon to double-check the rounds left over from the parking lot shootout, she slammed it back into place and removed the safety. Finger beside the trigger, Ana retraced her steps toward the kitchen. Then slowed as cold air brushed against her face.

The sliding glass door hadn't been open when she'd gone to check on Olivia.

A soft protest of wood flooring from behind spun her around just as a wall of muscle slammed into her. The cabin blurred in her vision a split second before her head snapped back onto the floor. Hand tight on the gun, she took aim at the masked attacker, finger over the trigger.

But faster than Ana thought possible, he clamped his hand over the barrel of the weapon and twisted until the sound of crunching bone and splintering pain was all she knew. Her groan drowned the rough inhales and exhales coming from beneath her attacker's mask, but she wasn't down yet. Hiking her knee into his kidneys, she used his own momentum to slam him into the floor face-first. Disoriented, he gave her enough time to latch on to the glass coffee table and shove to her feet.

The bedroom door swung open, and Benning's daughter stepped into the moonlight.

"Olivia, no! Run—" Searing pain spread across her scalp as the bastard fisted a handful of her hair and threw her back into the wall that made up the oversize fireplace. The air slammed out of her lungs, but she didn't have time to recover. She dodged the fist aimed directly at her face as he rocketed his knuckles into the stone behind her. Targeting her shoulder into his midsection, she threw everything she had into hiking her attacker off his feet. She couldn't let him get to Olivia. Her stitches pulled tight. She locked her back teeth against the scream working up her throat but didn't make it so much as a single step forward before a direct hit to her bullet wound knocked her off balance. They both collapsed, both fought for air, but pain-induced nausea kept Ana down.

Her attacker stood over her, a hint of sweat and new car smell working deep into her lungs. This wasn't some run-of-the-mill criminal set on covering up a murder. The way he moved, the way he'd targeted her wound. He was a professional. Former military, or at least trained in advanced maneuvers, and he'd put Benning and his family in his sights. "You weren't supposed to get involved, Agent Ramirez."

"Congratulations, you've done your homework and figured out who I am." Shaking her head, she clamped a hand over her side and struggled to her feet, only to collapse again. Blood soaked through her cookie dough-stained shirt. *Mierda*. Would she have any clothes left by the time this case was over? She forced her breathing to slow and swallowed the dryness in her throat. Steel resolve pulled her shoulders back, and she settled her gaze on her attacker's. She'd made Benning a promise. She'd given him her word to protect him, protect Olivia and bring Owen home. She wasn't about to fail him now. "What I want to know is who the hell are you? And where's Benning?"

A hollow laugh filtered through the pounding behind her ears. In less than two moves, he dropped the magazine from her service weapon and disassembled the gun. Pocketing the magazine, he tossed the rest, the sound of metal on wood a shock straight to her nerves.

"I know you, Ramirez. I used to be you, so believe me when I say it'd be in your best interest to walk away while you still can." He shot his hand out, gripping her throat and hauling her into his muscled chest. Her heart threatened to punch through her rib cage as he squeezed hard enough to constrict her airway. He cocked his head to one side, revealing a line of flawless skin between the ski mask and his leather jacket. He braced his feet apart as she struggled with both hands around his wrist. "Mr. Reeves took something that didn't belong to him, and now I'm the one who has to clean up the mess, but I wanted to give you a choice. For old time's sake. Give me the skull, hand over Benning Reeves and I'll let you live, or count yourself among the casualties when I'm done."

The skull. He didn't have it. Which meant someone else had taken it from the fireplace. Not the killer. Not Benning. Then who?

"Give me… Owen, and… I'll let you…live." Her eyes watered, that dark gaze blurring in her vision. Or was it the lack of oxygen making her dizzy? Didn't matter. In another thirty seconds—maybe a minute—none of this would matter. She had to stay awake, had to keep him from reaching Olivia, give Benning and his daughter a chance to run.

"I take it you're declining my offer," he said.

She dug her fingernails into her attacker's skin, drawing blood. His grip faltered, and Ana took advantage. Releasing her hands from his wrists, she struck his knee as hard as she could with her heel, and he dropped. She wrapped her hand and wrist close to his ear and used her weight to slam the side of his head into the floor. Her throat burned as she breathed, the muscles alongside her neck already sore. "I take it you haven't done nearly as much research on me as you should have."

A glint of moonlight off metal was all she noted before pain sliced across her arm. Her body twisted with the swipe of the blade, giving her attacker enough time to close the distance between them. Targeting her midsection, he hefted her off her feet, his arms locked around her waist. Ana jabbed her elbow into the sensitive bundle of nerves at the base of his spine as he pushed her backward. Once. Twice. Pain exploded through her lower back as he rammed her into the island countertop, and her laptop crashed to the floor. She blocked the hit aimed for the right side of her jaw, but the second swing came in too fast. She hit the floor. Hard.

"I didn't want it to end like this, Ramirez." His footsteps reverberated off the old wood flooring as her attacker took position above her. "You were one of the good ones until you put your own selfish needs over saving that poor girl."

Samantha Perry? How did he—

Lightning spread through her. Every breath, every

movement on her part, taught her a new lesson in pain tolerance. Raising her head, she caught sight of her discarded service weapon. He'd stripped it down, removed the magazine, but she wouldn't give up. The front door swung inward on its hinges, cold leaking into the cabin. Olivia had gotten away, but for how long? Alone, unarmed, unprotected, the girl wouldn't last the night on her own out there in the woods. Blood dripped from her nose, the taste of salt and copper filling her mouth as she reached for her gun only a few feet away. "I'm not dead…yet."

"Then let's get to it, shall we?" Ripping her off the floor, he dragged her toward the floor-to-ceiling windows looking out over the north side of the cabin and spun her back into the glass. The window vibrated along her spine, cracks spidering outward, and her blood pressure spiked higher. "Nothing personal, Ramirez. You used to be a good agent, just not good enough to beat me."

He landed a hard kick to her stomach, and the window shattered, sending her into darkness.

THE CRUNCH OF footsteps in snow pierced through the haze in his head.

Benning pulled his chin from his chest, but his head hit something solid. Pain exploded down his neck. Son of a… Sections of his shoulder-length hair caught in his beard. What the hell happened? His shoulders ached, the cold working into his joints, but that wasn't what was stopping him from moving his arms. He'd been tied against a tree, with rope from the feel of it. Who—

He'd been chopping wood to distract himself after accusing Ana of being nothing more than a shell of the woman he'd fallen in love with. Regret for what he'd said had only served to push him harder, torn open the gaping wound he'd struggled to plug since she'd left. Obviously without success. He'd heard something move in the trees. Then there'd been nothing but darkness. He'd been hit from behind. Someone had knocked him unconscious. Someone knew they were here.

"Your son is running out of time, Mr. Reeves." Motion-detecting lights cast the man in front of him into shadow, a ski mask covering the bastard's face. Snow crunched under heavy footfalls as his attacker crouched in front of him. Gravel coated the man's voice, but instant recognition threw Benning back to the night Owen and Olivia had been taken. It was him, the man who'd pointed a gun at him on that construction site and abducted his son. "I gave you twenty-four hours to hand over what you took from the site, and now you've forced me to do something I don't want to do." The cabin's outdoor lights reflected off a jagged-edged blade, stained with some dark substance along the blade—blood?—and Benning leveraged his feet into the snow. "Where is the skull?"

"I don't have it." Truth. But apparently, neither did the SOB in front of him. Agent Cantrell had been right. Someone had gotten to the skull before the Tactical Crime Division had. Spitting the thick coating in his mouth into the snow, he set his head back against the tree. His head throbbed with his racing heartbeat. He tugged at the ropes around his wrists, but there wasn't any give. "I can tell you one thing. The second I get out of these ropes, I'm going to kill you for taking my son."

Lightning exploded as the bastard's fist connected with one side of his jaw. His eyes watered, blood filling his mouth as the trees, the outline of the man in front of him, everything blurred.

"You know, Ana Sofia threatened me with the same end." His attacker leaned in, the scent of new car smell and soap heavy in the air. "Right before I threw her through a window."

No. That wasn't possible. Ana wasn't dead. Couldn't be. She was a federal agent. She'd been trained to fight, to protect the innocent. Nothing—not even the bastard in front of him or anything Benning had accused her of—could bring her down. Heat spread from behind his sternum as seconds ticked by, the muscles along his jaw protesting. Shaking his head, he let the tree bark bite into the wound from where he'd been knocked unconscious. She wasn't dead. Because that meant... That meant he'd never get to tell her he hadn't meant what he'd said. "You're lying."

"Are you really willing to take that chance? Are you willing to bet your daughter's life on it?" His attacker pressed cold steel against Benning's face, and the muscles across his back tensed. "Because without Agent Ramirez protecting her, there's nothing stopping me from doing to her what I plan to do to Owen once your twenty-four hours runs out." The edge of the blade pierced through the thin skin at his cheek, a drop of blood trickling down from the cut. "The skull, Mr. Reeves. That's all I want, and you and your kids can go back to your lives and forget I ever existed."

He wasn't part of this world. He wasn't trained in hand-to-hand combat, weapons or negotiation. He didn't come into contact with killers on a daily basis like Ana and the rest of the Tactical Crime Division, but even Benning recognized the lie behind the promise. He forced his fingers to uncurl and plunged them into the snow behind the tree, out of sight. There had to be something—anything—he could use to cut himself free. He just needed more time. His finger brushed against a sharp edge of a rock. Not sharp enough to break skin, but he hoped like hell it would do the job. Setting the rock against what he thought was the thinnest section of rope, Benning worked to cut through the braided fibers as fast as he could. "Tell me whose body the FBI pulled from the fireplace on my property."

"Your new friends at TCD haven't ID'd her yet?" He shook his head. "Pity what had to go down. It was nothing personal, but your nanny took her job a little too seriously, watching those kids."

Jo. Dread fisted in the pit of his stomach. "She didn't have anything to do with this."

"You're the one who brought her into this when you removed the skull from that site, Mr. Reeves. Not me. Her blood is on your hands. Just as Agent Ramirez's, and just like it will be when I find your daughter." His attacker straightened, the weight of those dark eyes pressurizing the air in his lungs. If this guy had beat Ana as he'd claimed, he'd been trained. There was no way Benning could compete with that, but he sure as hell wasn't going to go down without a fight. Not with his daughter unprotected. Not with his son missing, and not with Ana injured— possibly dying—somewhere out here. "You're stalling."

"Yes, I am." Benning cut through the last of the ropes at his wrists and launched forward, taking the bastard by surprise. He aimed to return the hit to his jaw, but his attacker dodged the attack and used his own momentum to unbalance him and slammed another fist into his face. Benning stumbled backward, then shot out another punch, making contact. Bracing his feet apart, he lifted his hands into position as his head threatened to split down the middle. He caught the SOB's wrist as the blade swung down toward him but left his midsection open. One hit. Another. The air crushed from his lungs as the man in the mask took advantage, and Benning had to release his hold on the knife in order to protect himself. The blade sliced down his arm, the sting drawing a gasp from between his teeth, but for a split second, the movement left his attacker open. He wrapped one forearm around the bastard's neck and hauled him back off his feet. Only he hadn't anticipated the elbow straight back into his gut. His grip loosened as pain exploded through his side, and he let the man in the mask free.

The killer caught Benning's wrist and twisted it behind him. His shoulder socket screamed right before a knee rocketed into Benning's face.

His vision went dark. He hit the ground, snow working under his shirt and into his boots. Every cell in his body begged him to stay down, to give up. It'd be easy, but this wasn't how this would end. He wasn't going to leave his kids' lives in the hands of a killer. He wasn't going to let Ana's sacrifice be for nothing.

"You don't know when to give up, do you? But I'll tell you the same thing I told Ana before I sent her to her death. You can't beat me. I've lost once before, and I'm not about to let it happen again." Movement registered above him, a shadow casting across his face. "Now, I'm going to give you one last chance to tell me where you hid the skull you took from the construction site before I lose my patience and put a bullet between your eyes, just as I did to him."

His breath sawed in and out of his lungs. Leveraging his palms into the snow, Benning struggled to his feet. His vision cleared. Exhaustion and pain tore through him, but he braced his legs wide. Ready to finish this once and for all. "I'm going to keep my word about killing you."

Benning kicked out, landing his boot heel center mass, then struck out with a right hook, followed by a left. Adrenaline dumped into his veins, throwing the pain and exhaustion into the back of his mind where it belonged. His knuckles met bone twice more before the bastard blocked his third attempt. The next fist made contact to the left side of his head, disorienting him. Benning stumbled back and slammed into the tree he'd been tied to seconds before. Sliding down the bark, he battled to stay upright as the man in the mask landed one hit after the other. His head twisted after each strike. He couldn't block the punches. They were coming too fast. Too hard.

"Leave my daddy alone!" The familiar voice sent panic through his system. Blood dripped from one eyebrow as his eye swelled shut, but Benning didn't mistake Olivia's small frame running as fast as her legs could carry her toward him.

"Olivia…" The brutal attack from the man above him ceased as the bastard turned his attention on his daughter. Suddenly, the physical pain, the exhaustion, the haze closing in, it all disappeared. A growl tore from his throat. "No!"

His son had already been taken from him. Ana had come back into his life only to be ripped away. The SOB wouldn't take Olivia, too. Ever.

His daughter swung the tree branch between both hands at his attacker as hard as she could, but her target stopped the attack before she could make contact. Ripping the makeshift weapon from her hands, the man in the mask advanced. Olivia tripped, landing on her rear, bright blue eyes widening in terror.

"Stay the hell away from her." Benning used everything he had left to get to his feet. The ground threatened to fall right out from under him, but he used the temporary rush of adrenaline to stay upright. "Your fight is with me."

"You're right." His attacker pivoted, keeping both Benning and Olivia in his peripheral vision on either side of him. One second. Two. In the blink of an eye, the shooter withdrew a gun from his low back and took aim at Benning. "It's time to put an end to it."

He pulled the trigger.

Olivia's scream echoed in his head as Benning collapsed to his knees. "Daddy!"

Chapter Seven

The gunshot ripped her from unconsciousness in blinding fury.

A gasp tore from her throat as the reality of what'd happened closed in, second by second. The intruder, the fight, the window. Ana tucked her chin to her chest, trying to sit up. A large piece of glass pierced straight through her thigh. A soft whimper escaped from between her lips as she tested the injury with one hand. *Hijo de perra.* She collapsed her head back into the snow, barely registering her stiff joints and muscles. How long had she been out here, unconscious? She searched the sky, the sun well behind the Smokeys. The only source of dim light came from the motion-detecting spotlights around the corner of the cabin, which ran off batteries instead of the main power or generator. But that gunshot had come from nearby. Tears burned in her eyes. "Damn it, Benning."

No. She swallowed the sob building in her throat. Emotions led to mistakes. Mistakes risked lives. She had to get up, had to find him, find Olivia. Given the fact she was conscious, the glass must not have cut through an artery, but she couldn't take the chance of removing it without cutting off blood supply first— just in case. Okay. She had to use something as a tourniquet, then take care of the wound. Should be relatively easy. She'd been shot less than twenty-four hours ago, and it hadn't stopped her from doing her job. A piece of window in her leg wouldn't slow her down, either. She locked her back teeth in an effort to distract her from the pain. "Get up, Ramirez. You're not finished."

Leveraging her weight into her elbows, she searched her surroundings and caught sight of her SUV parked in the driveway along the other side of the cabin. There had to be something inside she could use. Rope, a bungee cord. Something. Thirty feet. She could make it thirty feet. Her exhales didn't crystallize in front of her mouth, her body temperature dropping too fast, but she couldn't worry about that right now. She had to make it. There were no other options. Not for Benning, and not for his family. She stretched one arm out above her head and slowly rolled onto her side, careful not to nudge the sharp tip of glass that'd cut straight through her. One hand pressing into the ground, she balanced with the other until she'd put nearly all of her weight into her uninjured leg and straightened. A wave of black washed over her vision, gravity doing everything in its power to bring her back to earth, and she had to force herself to breathe through the pain in her side. "Move, damn it."

One step. Then another. Blood slid down the inside of her pants. She only pushed herself harder. The faster her heart raced, the faster she'd bleed out, but she'd take that risk if it meant getting to Benning in time. She wasn't going to deny the ache she'd had to live with since that night she'd slipped from his bed and disappeared. Throwing herself into her work hadn't helped. Making herself numb to emotion or caring about the people around her—the people she saved—hadn't helped. Nothing had. Until he'd kissed her.

It'd been reckless and dangerous and wrong, but she hadn't done anything to fight it. She'd laid out the rules in no uncertain terms when it came to what'd happened between them, but in that moment Benning had broken past the defenses she'd taken so long to build with a single sweep of his tongue past her lips. Just as he'd always been able to do. He'd stirred things inside her she hadn't let herself feel in so long, and there'd been nothing she'd wanted more. In those few seconds she'd been stripped bare, left raw and exposed to the truth. That she… She'd been in love with him, too. She'd denied how she'd felt in the name of saving lives, when deep down the real reason had been festering all along.

She couldn't take the pain of losing anyone else.

Not after losing her baby sister at two years old, not after failing to recover Samantha Perry before her body was found decimated in that alley. She'd ensured she'd never have to feel that grief again by leaving behind the one man who'd undeniably break her into a thousand pieces if given the chance in order to protect herself. Benning.

She wasn't going to die out here. Not until she fulfilled her promise.

Using the exterior of the cabin as a stabilizer, Ana hobbled toward the SUV as fresh snow fell from the sky. Her lungs burned, nausea churning in her stomach. She'd already lost so much blood it felt as though ice sludged through her veins, but the pressure of being exposed—out in the open—took priority. Her attacker had taken her gun and nearly her life. She could only do something about one of those things right now. Twisting her head around the corner of the cabin, mere feet from the SUV, she listened for movement, waited for the next ambush. Only the pounding of her own heart behind her ears registered. Exhaustion compelled her to rest here, to close her eyes and wait until her strength returned, but time was running out. She had no idea who that gunshot had been meant for, if Benning was alive, or if Olivia had gotten to safety. And as long as she was conscious, she'd fight to find out.

"Now or never, Ramirez." She took a few deep breaths, the burn in her lungs a dull piercing now. Blood was still leeching from the wound across her pant leg. It hadn't slowed, which meant the piece of glass wasn't doing a great job holding her together.

Benning wasn't the only one out of time. "You didn't come all this way for nothing."

She searched the side of the house one more time. Then ran.

A bullet ripped past her left arm, an inch—maybe two—from her heart as she lunged for the tail of the SUV, but she had to keep moving. Her leg dragged behind her, her toes and calf muscles numb. Two more shots embedded in the side of the cabin and another in the passenger-side door of her vehicle as she took cover. Out of breath and ideas, she pulled her injured leg behind the SUV and closed her eyes as another four rounds exploded through the night. *Hostia.* Bloody hell. She pressed her neck and back into the vehicle's bumper and got to her feet, compressing the hatch's lever. Locked. The breath rushed out of her as she scooped a fist-size rock from the snow and shattered the back windshield. She cleared glass from the bottom track, discarded the rock, and opened the hatch from the inside. Crawling inside, she bit back the urge to scream as the glass shifted in her thigh, and she closed the gate behind her. She was hidden. At least temporarily. It wouldn't do much considering she'd left a trail of blood and glass in her wake, but none of this would matter unless she got the bleeding under control. If she was going to get Benning and Olivia the hell out of here, she had to focus. "Okay, okay. If I were a piece of rope, where would I be?"

Tossing extra raincoats, flares and spare water

bottles from the emergency kit, she dumped the rest of the contents into the SUV's cargo space and nearly collapsed back in relief. She grabbed the single bungee cord, still in its package, from the mess. Closing her eyes, Ana set her back against the second row of seats. She prepared herself for the pain that was coming before pinching the glass between both sets of fingers. She sucked in a deep breath. Pressing her heels into the vehicle's floor, she locked her back teeth to keep from giving away her position. "Like a Band-Aid. Nothing you haven't survived before."

She pulled the large piece of glass entirely through her leg with everything she had left, then tossed it aside. Reaching for the bungee cord, she discarded the packaging and wrapped the braided fibers tight around her leg, above the wound. She slammed her head back into the row of seats as pain exploded through her. Tingling sensations shot like lightning down through her calves and toes as feeling rocketed back into her nerves. Darkness closed in around the edges of her vision, but she had to stay awake. Had to get to Benning.

"I know you're in there, Ramirez." Snow crunched beneath heavy footsteps outside the vehicle. "And from the trail you're leaving behind, it looks like you're not in very good shape."

A knot swelled in the pit of her stomach.

Sifting through the supplies she'd dumped across the cargo space, she gripped a screwdriver. The bright orange head faded in and out of focus as she tried to pry open a hidden storage panel beside the tailgate. The plastic cover finally fell away, and she wrapped her hand around the backup piece she'd stored before she'd left TCD headquarters. Always be prepared. That was what her brothers had taught her from the time she'd been five years old. That, and how to disassemble a gun so it'd fit inside any small storage compartment. She made quick work of assembling the pieces into place and loading the magazine as the footsteps pierced through the pounding in her head. "Only eight more lives left. Don't suppose that means you're going to cut me some slack—"

Gunshots exploded from outside. Blood burst across the tinted side window of the SUV, and the large outline of a man fell against the side of the vehicle. Ana fell back onto her side and raised her weapon. Waiting. Tension stretched across her shoulders as the seconds ticked by. Maybe a full minute. Slower than her instincts told her to go, she unlatched the tailgate and slid out of the vehicle, gun in hand. Her breath shuddered in her chest. She swung around to the passenger side of the vehicle, ready to pull the trigger.

But no one was there. Only a trail of blood—separate from hers—and a larger set of footprints led away from her position and into the trees.

"Ana." Movement registered from behind, and she twisted around and took aim.

At a familiar face.

"Benning." She released the breath she hadn't realized she'd been holding, adjusting her grip around her weapon. Her hands shook, the pain in her leg the only thing keeping her in the moment. She lowered the gun to her side as a sob nearly broke through her control.

Just before she collapsed.

"ANA!" HIS BLOOD ran cold, heart jerking in his chest. Lungs emptied of oxygen as a different kind of pain exploded through him. Benning pushed his legs as hard as he could to catch her before she hit the ground. But he wasn't fast enough. His boots slid across an iced-over patch of snow, bringing him to his knees, but it couldn't stop him. Nothing would stop him from getting to her. Clawing through snow, he discarded the gun he'd taken from her duffel bag inside the cabin after he'd woken and slipped his uninjured arm around her limp body. Fresh blood dripped from her nose and mouth, her skin too pale. He pressed his index and middle finger to the base of her throat, and a rush of relief flooded through him. Her heartbeat pulsed against his finger, slow, thready, but there. "Come on, Ana, open your eyes. Look at me."

No response.

Hauling her upper body out of the snow, he gritted through the pain in his shoulder and skimmed the pad of his thumb across the bluish tint in her lips. The bastard who'd shot him had run before Benning had gotten another shot off, but it was the bright red

stain of blood that had pooled beneath her, such a
sharp contrast in the snow, that hiked his blood pressure higher now. Hell, she looked like she'd gone four
rounds with a professional boxer and been stabbed in
the process. He had to get her inside. Had to get her
warm. He brought her into his chest, then scanned
the tree line twenty feet to the north. The bullet to
his shoulder had taken him down for a few minutes,
and when he'd come back around, the shooter and
his daughter were gone. Where was Olivia? Every
muscle down his spine tightened with battle-ready
tension, and Benning shook the woman in his arms.
"Ana, wake up. You have to get up. You have to tell
me where Olivia is."

He'd searched the cabin after he'd woken alone
in the snow. No one—not even the bastard who'd
attacked him—had been inside. Which meant his
daughter was somewhere out here or…or the killer
had taken her, too. If the same man who'd tied him
to a tree was responsible for taking his son, the SOB
had made a grave mistake. Benning set his hand over
Ana's heart, blood crusting to her angled features.
The skull was still out there. Benning didn't know
where, or who had taken it from the fireplace, but
he'd be damn sure the shooter never got his hands
on it.

"Benning." His name struggled past her lacerated
lips, barely a whisper over the constant whine of the
wind through the trees.

He fisted her T-shirt in his hands and pulled her

upright. Desperation and hints of anger bled into his voice. "Ana, where is Olivia? I need to know what happened to my daughter."

"I couldn't stop him." Hazel-green eyes struggled to focus on him. Her hands fell limp at her sides, and for the first time he noted her bloodied knuckles and what looked like a knife wound across the top of her arm. "I tried, but I wasn't strong enough. I screamed at her to run. I don't know where she is."

"You told her to run?" He loosened his grip on her shirt, and everything—the darkening bruising around her throat, the busted lip, the torn stitches, and her black-and-blue index finger—rushed into focus. Sweat sheened across her flawless skin, dark circles more prominent than a minute ago. He recovered the gun he'd dropped and shoved the barrel down the back of his jeans. "Hang on to me."

A groan ripped from his throat as he hauled her into his chest and got to his feet, and the hollow space behind his sternum ripped wider. In these temperatures, combined with the loss of blood, her body was bordering on hypothermia and shock. He'd prioritized his daughter's life over hers.

Without Ana, he and Olivia would already be dead. He owed her his life.

His legs burned as they climbed the stairs, maneuvered her through the sliding glass door and swung her down onto the nearest couch in the living room. First-aid kit. He'd left it on the kitchen table after stitching her the first time, but first, he had to get her core temperature back up. Ripping every blanket he could find from the beds, he dashed back into the living room to find her struggling to her feet. "What are you doing? You've lost a lot of blood, but stitches aren't going to do a damn bit of good if you die from hypothermia."

"You know you're bleeding, too, right?" Heavy eyelids drooped lower as she shuffled toward him.

"Bastard shot me after Olivia attacked him. Now I don't know where she is. At least I can say I shot him back." But the man in the mask had slipped away before Benning could get the answers he needed. The echo of Olivia's scream still played in his head, the memory of the suspect advancing on his daughter fresh. The cut on the back of his head throbbed. "Now, get back on that couch so I can keep you alive."

"She's a smart girl, Benning. We're going to find her." Ana fell against the kitchen table, strands of beautiful dark hair sticking to her skin and neck. Her gasp destroyed the lingering effects of their last conversation and pressurized the air in his lungs. "I promised I would keep your daughter safe, and that's exactly what I'm going to do. Right after we take care of that wound of yours."

"Damn it, Ana." He lunged forward before she hit the floor. Taking her weight, he settled her back against his chest as he slowly lowered them both to the hardwood. Her skin was hot, sweat slicking down the side of her temples despite having been discarded in the snow for who knew how long. "How the hell are you going to do that when you can't even stand?"

"I'm not going to lose you again, Benning." Long lashes rested against the tops of her cheeks as she closed her eyes, but when she opened them again, a fire he'd never seen before burned in the depths. "And I'm not going to lose her, too. I can't."

Her voice broke, right along with his heart. Something shifted then. Something he couldn't explain as she rested against him. He'd been wrong before. She'd detached herself from the people she'd been assigned to find, but not because she didn't want to feel the pain and loss of another victim, someone she cared about. How hadn't he seen it before now? It'd been there in the way she'd kept her bullet wound to herself to get them to safety, the way she'd shouldered the blame of Samantha Perry's death, how she'd sacrificed herself to give his daughter a chance to run. Even now, she was determined to put his medical needs above her own, despite the fact she was on the verge of passing out.

She wasn't protecting herself from being hurt again.

She was punishing herself.

For what'd happened to her sister, what'd happened to Samantha Perry seven years ago. All of it. She'd taken the blame and twisted it into her own personal responsibility, leaving her wrung out and nothing more than the empty shell he'd accused her of becoming. She'd cut herself off from the things—

the people—she cared about the most, not because they were a distraction, but because she didn't believe she deserved them to be part of her life. That because she'd failed, she didn't deserve to be cared for. Benning swept her hair out of her face. He held her tighter, counted her slowing inhales and exhales. No. She wasn't going to die here. Her lashes dipped to the tops of her cheeks once again, and his eyes burned with the possibility of losing her all over again. "You're not a ghost of the woman I fell in love with. I was wrong. I know now why you left, why you think you need to put your own life on the line for everybody else to make up for the past, but if you keep going like this, you're not going to have anything left to give, Ana, and my kids need you." He took a deep breath as the truth surfaced. "I need you."

"It's my fault." Her voice vibrated against his chest. She struggled to open her eyes, her hands limp by her sides. "I was the one who was supposed to be watching my sister the day she went missing. I'm the one who should've found something we could use on Harold Wood before he killed that girl. No one else. Me."

Warmth spread through him as he set his cheek against the crown of her head.

"You were five years old when your sister was taken, Ana. Five. You couldn't have even saved yourself at that age, let alone someone else. You were a child, and nobody in their right mind blames you for what happened. Just as nobody blames you for what happened to Samantha Perry." Tension built at the thought of how many times she'd internalized that blame, made it a part of herself, carried it on her shoulders day after day, how it affected her life. Her happiness. "The criminals who abducted them, they're the ones who need to answer for their crimes. Not you. Don't you see that?"

She didn't answer.

"You told me the work you do makes it so you have to walk in the dark, and I believe you." He smoothed blood from her bottom lip, and a new level of awareness heightened his senses, chased back the pain in his shoulder. He shouldn't be surprised. She'd always had this effect on him, always been able to shut out the chaos around them, grounded him, kept him in the moment. Gave him confidence. "But nobody said you have to do it alone or that you don't deserve to see the light."

She shook her head. "I should've been able to save her."

"Think of how many others you have saved, Ana. They're alive because of you." He'd been down this road, blamed himself for not being strong enough to protect Owen and Olivia, but in the end, that wasn't what mattered. He could tell her it was because his kids were out there, possibly in the hands of a killer, that he'd laid it all out there, but that wouldn't be the truth. He cared about her. From the moment she'd walked onto that construction site asking him questions about the Samantha Perry case seven years ago, he'd known she was the kind of woman he wanted to spend the rest of his life with. She was intelligent, independent, insightful and caring when she let that part of herself show. And, damn it, she deserved more than this, more than a life filled with unanswered questions, heartache and pain. She deserved to be happy. He and the twins, they could make her happy. The thought should've scared him, but a sense of rightness, conviction, burned behind his sternum. Hadn't he'd always felt that way when it came to her? "This obsession you have with saving everyone but yourself only has one end. Yours." A hint of anger bled into his voice. "Damn it, Ana, you have people that care about you, but you're too consumed by your own mistakes to see it."

She hauled the gun off the floor and struggled to her feet, unstable. Eyes heavy, she limped toward the kitchen table and collapsed into the same chair she'd sat in as he'd stitched the wound in her side. "There are only two people I care about right now, and after you help me stitch up this wound, I'm going to find them."

Chapter Eight

She wiped crusted blood from her face, flashlight to the ground.

The power was still cut from the cabin, but they didn't have time to fix it now. Olivia was out here, in the cold and on the run. Whoever'd pushed Ana through that window would be on the girl's trail. Had maybe even caught up with her already. The thought exposed the very real fear climbing her spine, but she pushed forward, forcing her attacker's parting words to the back of her mind. She might not be strong enough to beat this particular threat, but she'd sure as hell slow him down. As for Benning… Whatever illusions he had about her would have to wait. The kidnapper had given them twenty-four hours to hand over the evidence Benning had pulled from that wall. They had three hours left until the deadline. Not enough time to recover the skull, find Olivia and save Owen, but Ana would fight until the end. "Over here."

Small footprints interrupted the smooth surface

of fresh snow between larger divots, heading south, away from the cabin and into the tree line. Olivia had gone out the cabin's front door after Ana had screamed at her to run, but according to Benning, the girl had attacked the shooter just before he'd put a bullet in Benning's shoulder and been gone when he'd woken. From the looks of it, she'd changed direction when she'd run and tried to hide her tracks by dragging something behind her. A smile tugged at one side of Ana's mouth. Good girl.

No fresh tire tracks interrupted the area around the cabin. Their attacker hadn't driven a vehicle straight up to the safe house. Too obvious. They would've heard him coming the moment he'd hit the head of the driveway, which meant he had to have come from the tree line. A snowmobile or an ATV? Either would get him on and off the property relatively quickly. Silence pressed on her from every direction. He had to know the area. Had to know the layout of the land and all the best places to attack from. He'd known exactly how to find them and when they'd been the most vulnerable.

Raising the flashlight to follow the trail, she struggled against the invisible lead in her legs as they headed into the woods. The hand-sewn stitches in her thigh wouldn't last long, but they'd have to do for now. Benning seemed to be handling the bullet in his shoulder. Or maybe desperation had finally caught up with him and the pain didn't matter.

"I can't decide if your daughter is a genius or if she's read too many mystery novels."

"Both." Benning kept a safe distance from behind, but she could still feel him on her skin. Could still feel his chest pressed against her back as he'd held on to her, remembered the vibration of his words against her spine, and her body heat hiked a few more degrees. Then again, it could be the shock of losing so much blood finally starting to take a toll. Either way, she had to focus, had to keep moving. Because the longer they were out here, the higher chance Olivia would succumb to the elements. "You should see her room. She's decorated it in crime-scene tape."

Benning helped her as she hauled her injured leg over a fallen tree, still following the trail in the snow. Her toes and fingers had already gone numb from dropping temperatures, and she couldn't imagine Olivia much better off. Had the girl even been wearing a jacket? Or shoes? Ana couldn't remember. Stabbing pain had dulled to an ache around the wound, but there was still a chance the glass had nicked something larger. The possibility of not making it out of these trees alive, of failing Olivia, Owen, Benning, just as she'd failed Samantha Perry, pushed her harder.

There wasn't a doubt in her mind she could've saved that girl if she'd been focused on doing her job and not the man at her side, but she couldn't get his admission out of her head. He needed her, cared about her. Not the emotionally isolated investigator she'd presented to her team and to the world, but the woman hiding behind the mistakes she'd made. The real her, the one he'd claimed he'd fallen in love with before her world had been ripped apart. She leaned into his hard frame for support. Did that woman even exist anymore? She wanted her to, if for nothing else than to shed the guilt that had taken control of her life for so long, to carve her own path. To be the kind of woman Benning would be proud to have in his and his kids' lives. The idea thickened the saliva in her mouth. She wasn't sure that future was a possibility anymore. Not for her. "You were right before."

This close, his body heat tunneled through her coat, and her exhales started crystallizing on the air as they moved as one. He took most of her weight, but even with the bullet in his shoulder, his control never broke. "About what?"

"I've been blinded by my mistakes. My...failures." The word turned bitter on her tongue. "I detached myself from the people who care about me, from everyone, because it was the easy thing to do." Her breath shuddered in her chest as they navigated through the trees. "I blamed myself for what happened to Samantha Perry. I thought since she didn't get to be with the people who loved her, the least I could do is put myself in the same position to try to make up for my mistake, which doesn't make sense, I know. But now I'm not sure redemption is an option. At least, not for me."

He slowed, staring down at her with that unread-

"One Minute" Survey

You get up to **FOUR books** <u>and</u> TWO Mystery Gifts...

Dear Reader,

Your opinions are important to us. So if you'll participate in our fa
and free "One Minute" Survey, **YOU** can pick up to four wonderfu
books that **WE** pay for!

As a leading publisher of women's fiction, we'd love to hear from
you. That's why we promise to reward you for completing our
survey.

IMPORTANT: Please complete the survey and return it. We'll sen
your Free Books and Free Mystery Gifts right away. **And we pay
for shipping and handling too!** *We pay for EVERYTHING!*

Try **Harlequin® Romantic Suspense** books featuring heart-racing
page-turners with unexpected plot twists and irresistible chemist
that will keep you guessing to the very end.

Try **Harlequin Intrigue® Larger-Print** books featuring action-pack
stories that will keep you on the edge of your seat. Solve the crim
and deliver justice at all costs.

Or TRY BOTH!

Thank you again for participating in our "One Minute"
Survey. It really takes just a minute (or less) to complete the
survey… and your free books and gifts will be well worth it!

Sincerely,

Pam Powers

Pam Powers
for Reader Service

"One Minute" Survey

GET YOUR FREE BOOKS AND FREE GIFTS!

✓ Complete this Survey ✓ Return this survey

1 Do you try to find time to read every day?
[ ] YES [ ] NO

2 Do you prefer stories with suspenseful storylines?
[ ] YES [ ] NO

3 Do you enjoy having books delivered to your home?
[ ] YES [ ] NO

4 Do you find a Larger Print size easier on your eyes?
[ ] YES [ ] NO

YES! I have completed the above "One Minute" Survey. Please send me my Free Books and Free Mystery Gifts (worth over $20 retail). I understand that I am under no obligation to buy anything, as explained on the back of this card.

[ ] I prefer Harlequin®
Romantic Suspense
240/340 HDL GNUS

[ ] I prefer Harlequin
Intrigue® Larger Print
199/399 HDL GNUS

[ ] I prefer BOTH
240/340 & 199/399
HDL GNWG

FIRST NAME   LAST NAME

ADDRESS

APT.#   CITY

STATE/PROV.   ZIP/POSTAL CODE

READER SERVICE—Here's how it works:

BUSINESS REPLY MAIL
FIRST-CLASS MAIL   PERMIT NO. 717   BUFFALO, NY

POSTAGE WILL BE PAID BY ADDRESSEE

READER SERVICE
PO BOX 1341
BUFFALO NY 14240-8571

NO POSTAGE
NECESSARY
IF MAILED
IN THE
UNITED STATES

▲ If offer card is missing write to: Reader Service, P.O. Box 1341, Buffalo, NY 14240-8531 or visit www.ReaderService.com ▲

able expression. Mountainous shoulders blocked moonlight filtering through the trees, but she didn't need to see him clearly to know what he was thinking. She'd memorized every angle of his features the first day they'd met, and while seven years had gone by, he hadn't changed much. He'd become part of her, and there was nothing—no one—who could change that. Least of all her. "Caring about someone doesn't limit your ability to do your job, Ana. It's because you're emotionally invested in the people you're assigned to protect and recover that makes you such a good agent."

He meant every word, conviction strong in his voice.

She raised her gaze with his. "You really believe that."

"Yeah, I do." His voice dipped into dangerous territory, the scent of pine and soap diving into her lungs as he inched closer. "I know you, and I know despite the effort you go through to prove nothing gets past that guard you've built, you're one of the strongest, most caring and competent women I've had the pleasure of knowing. Of all the agents I could've requested to recover my son, I chose you. Because you're all I need."

Her throat swelled. All he needed? "I—"

A scream turned her blood cold.

"Olivia." Benning ran toward the sound, his back slightly hunched as he clamped a hand on his wound in his shoulder.

The darkness seemed thicker then. She raced after him, every cell in her body focused on getting to his daughter. They'd made it about fifty yards—maybe a bit more—into the wilderness, but it sounded as though the scream had come from the cabin. The possibility they were walking straight into a trap crossed her mind, but she struggled through the snow in spite of that. They had to take the risk. Thin twigs and branches caught on her coat sleeve as she tried to keep up. She hit the button on the flashlight and threw them into complete blackness. If the shooter saw them coming, he might do something rash, irreversible. Sweat built along her hairline as she forced one foot in front of the other. The pain was back, stitches stretching with every step. She couldn't stop. She had to find Olivia, had to bring her brother home. Blood soaked through her jeans and T-shirt, but the clock hadn't stopped because she was on the verge of passing out.

They cleared the tree line. Motion-censored lights kicked on, blinding her for a split second. She raised her hand to block the light, and there, positioned near the stairs, Ana made out his outline. The man who'd kicked her through a second-story window waited, his weapon in hand. And beside him, the shape of a six-year-old girl who'd known nothing but fear and loss these past two days.

"Didn't think you had what it took to survive a fall like that, Ramirez." The way he said her name, as though they knew each other, grated on her nerves.

A gloved hand rested over Olivia's shoulder, pull-ing her into his side. "You're going to need to have more than that leg looked at when we're finished here, though."

"You say that like you think I'm going to let you walk away." Not happening. She raised her gun, tak-ing aim with both hands gripped on steel. Benning shifted beside her, but didn't protest the fact with one wrong move, one pull of the trigger, she might accidentally hit his daughter. Tension rolled off him in waves, but she'd promised to protect his girl. That was exactly what she was going to do. "Hand over the girl, give me the location on her brother and I'll consider not pulling the trigger."

The mask covering his face shifted as though he couldn't help but smile despite the brand-new bullet hole in his own shoulder, courtesy of Benning. The shooter fanned his gloved grip over his gun, and a rush of nervous energy shot down her spine. "Tell you what. I'll make you a deal. Seeing as how I don't particularly enjoy hurting kids, I'll make a trade. I'll give you the girl and the location of the son, in ex-change for Mr. Reeves."

"And what's to stop me from shooting you right now and putting an end to all of this?" she asked.

"Because I'm the only one who knows where the boy is." Slowly, the shooter reached into his pocket and extracted his phone. Turning the screen toward them, he tossed the device at her feet. "Kill me, and you kill Owen Reeves, Agent Ramirez. Is that what you want?"

Forcing herself to keep her expression blank, Ana braced her feet apart and picked up the phone. Her insides jerked as she recognized the little boy from the file Director Pembrook had handed to her less than twenty-four hours ago. Owen Reeves. The footage looked as though it'd come from a hidden camera tucked into a corner of a small, dark room. And there he was. Alone. Afraid. Tears cutting streaks through the dirt on his cheeks.

Benning in exchange for his children.

No. There had to be another way out of this. She just had to find it. Olivia's sobs broke through her racing thoughts. She shook her head to clear out the chaos, but the answer was there, right on the tip of her tongue. The bastard had been playing games with them this entire time. Bringing the Samantha Perry case into this, leaving the charm at the crime scene on Benning's property, destroying evidence. He was trying to manipulate her. Offering a deal had to be another move in a long line of manipulation he'd put into play from the beginning, and she couldn't let herself fall for it. "No. No deal—"

"I'll do it," Benning said.

Her heart plummeted as she realized he'd seen the footage from the phone. She couldn't take her eyes off the shooter but kept Benning in her peripheral vision. This was not up for discussion. "No. We will figure this out together. The second he gets what he wants from you, he'll come back for your children to cover his tracks, and I'm not going to let that happen. My job is to protect you—"

"Your job is to recover my son." Benning tossed the gun he'd taken from her duffel bag a few feet away. Hands raised in surrender, he stepped away from her, toward the shooter. Shoulder-length hair hid his features as he increased the distance between them. "I'm counting on you to do it."

ONE STEP AT a time. Benning tensed as the bastard holding his daughter hostage slid his hand off her shoulder. With a nudge, the man who'd shot him forced her forward but kept in line with Olivia's every move. The weight of Ana's attention from behind tunneled through his coat and under his skin. His heart rate throbbed around the site of the new hole in his shoulder, but knowing she'd be the one protecting Olivia and that she'd do whatever it took to find Owen, eased the uncertainty tearing through him. The SOB behind the mask hadn't given him a choice. Not really. This was the only way to ensure his mistake didn't haunt his children forever. The spotlights positioned around the cabin reflected off the tears streaking down Olivia's face as he closed in on her. "It's going to be okay, baby. Ana's going to watch you for a little bit until I can come get you. Okay? Everything's going to be fine."

"Daddy, I want to go home." Her sob broke through her tough personality, and she suddenly became the defenseless, vulnerable little girl he'd held after she'd been born, who'd cried until he'd picked her up.

"You're going home, Liv. You just have to be strong for a little bit longer. This will all be over soon. I promise." The words choked in his throat. He'd never lied to his kids, but this lie had slid from his mouth easily enough. He wasn't coming home. Ana was right. As soon as the shooter got ahold of the skull Benning had taken from that wall, all of this would be over, and his children will have lost both parents before they turned seven. But he couldn't watch them suffer for his sins any longer. Not when he could end this nightmare right now. Curling his hands into fists to keep himself from reaching out for her—to keep himself from doubting his decision— he faced the bastard who'd ripped his family apart. "You can take your hands off my daughter now."

Wrenching free, Olivia ran straight for him and wrapped her arms around his neck as he crouched to catch her weight. "No, Daddy! No. You have to come with me."

"So very touching," the shooter said. "But I'm starting to run out of patience, Mr. Reeves. The more time you waste here, the less time your son has."

His heart threatened to shatter into a thousand pieces right there in the snow between a federal agent and an armed gunman. He turned slightly, and, raising his gaze to meet Ana's, he straightened with his daughter in his arms. This wasn't how it was supposed to be. "You have to go with Ana now, Liv. You have to go. I love you, but you have to go."

"You can do this, Olivia." Ana kept her gun trained on his kids' kidnapper, every bit the federal agent he'd relied on to get him and his twins through this. "Think of all those times the investigators in your favorite books had to make a hard choice, but in the end, the hard choice is what moves the story forward and solves the case, isn't it? Otherwise, the characters wouldn't find out how strong they really are."

Olivia unwrapped her arms from around his neck. She sniffled, her big blue eyes holding on to unshed tears, but he couldn't release her. Not yet. "Yes."

"In the end, the investigator always gets the bad guy, right?" Ana glanced toward him, a single nod all the warning she gave him a split second before understanding hit. She wasn't talking about him or Olivia. She hobbled between the shooter and Benning, weapon raised. "They always get justice."

"You're making a mistake, Agent Ramirez." The shooter took a single step forward. "If I leave empty-handed, Owen isn't the only one who will suffer."

"I've made a lot of mistakes over my career. This isn't going to be one of them." Her shoulders rose and fell on steady inhales. Right before she pulled the trigger.

Benning twisted away from the fight, his hold on his daughter tight. Pumping his legs as hard as he could, he took cover behind one of the trees with

Ana close on his trail. Bark exploded to his right as
a bullet impacted mere inches from his head, and he
slid to his knees, shoving Olivia behind him. Ana
pressed her back into the tree beside him. "What the
hell are you doing? He's the only one who can tell
us where Owen is!"

"He was never going to reveal that information,
Benning. He's a killer. Killers only want one thing—
to keep from getting caught." She returned fire as the
SOB took cover behind the pile of firewood Benning
had been chopping that stood between them and their
only way out of here. The SUV. "Wherever Owen is,
there's too much evidence that could point back to
him. The only way to find your son is to identify the
owner of the skull you pulled out of that wall, and we
can't do that here." She fired another three rounds,
then the gun clicked empty. They were out of am-
munition. Tossing her weapon, she double-checked
the shooter's position. Pain contorted her features as
she placed both hands against her thigh, and his heart
jerked in his chest. "We have to get to the SUV."

"How?" Damn it. She wasn't in any condition to
go up against this guy again. Neither of them was.
He bit back the agony tearing through his shoulder.
Olivia huddled into his side as another bullet ripped
past them.

"There's nowhere you can run, Mr. Reeves," the
man in the mask said. "Nowhere you can hide that
I won't find you. One way or another, I will recover

what you took from me, and when I do, I'm going to enjoy what comes after."

"This guy is so full of himself, but he is the one with the gun." She shook her head, keeping tabs on their attacker. "Do you trust me?"

Benning slowed his hand's path along Olivia's back. Despite the fact Ana had walked away from him all those years ago, she'd nearly died protecting his daughter from the madman on the other side of that woodpile, stepped between him and a loaded gun and calmed Olivia through this whole thing. Trust her? Hell. He'd take another bullet if that was what she needed of him. "Yes."

"Then I'm going to go for the gun you tossed when you decided to surrender yourself over to this psychopath." She shoved the phone the shooter had handed over into her coat pocket. Her voice remained level despite the lack of color in her face and the fact her hands were shaking as she repositioned herself behind the tree. "When I give you the signal, you and Olivia make a run for the SUV. A spare set of keys are in the glove compartment. The SUV has a tracking device. My team will be able to find you."

Warning screamed through his system. "Ana, wait. You don't know how many rounds are left in that gun. You'll be exposed for however long it takes you to find where I dropped it."

She crossed the open space between the trees they'd taken cover behind, staying low. Another bullet flew over their heads, but with those mesmerizing hazel-green eyes locked on his, the world around the three of them disappeared. "No matter what happens, I need you to promise me you won't come back for me. Take your daughter and get as far from here as you can. Understand?"

Blood drained from his face and neck as her words registered. She didn't think she was going to make it out of here alive. "Ana, no. You're not—"

"Yes, I am." Fisting her hands in his T-shirt, she crushed her mouth to his. She pierced the seam of his lips with her tongue, and, for a brief moment, they were back in the cabin. Her covered in cookie dough, him desperate to taste her one more time. In those short seconds, everything had felt so…right between them. As though she'd never left. He'd been complete. But sooner than he wanted, Ana pulled away, and the cold crept back in. Releasing her grip from his shirt, she stood as best she could with the wound in her thigh. "You promised Olivia she could tour TCD headquarters when this was over."

He hugged his daughter tighter as he stared up at the woman who'd saved his life, saved his family. "Thank you."

"Don't come back for me." She took a deep breath, almost steeling herself, and charged from the tree line.

Gunfire exploded around them as Benning hauled himself and Olivia to his feet and raced as fast as he could through the trees. His daughter's weight tugged on the bullet wound in his shoulder as snow threatened to trip him every step of the way. He couldn't look back, couldn't slow down as his daughter's tears soaked into his neckline, couldn't stop the hole in his chest from splintering wider. His instincts screamed for him to turn around, but Ana had ordered him to get Olivia as far from here as possible. He had to keep going. He had to leave her behind. He curled his hands tighter in his daughter's pajamas. This was the choice Ana had asked him to make. "We're almost there, baby. Close your eyes. We're almost there."

Olivia beat against his back with her small hands. "Daddy, we have to go back! Ana needs our help! Go back!"

"We can't go back, Liv." His eyes burned at her pleas. His daughter wasn't the only one who'd gotten attached to the federal agent assigned to recover his son, but he'd keep his promise. The SUV came into view, and Benning left the protection of the trees. The back window had been shattered, glass crunching under his boots as he rounded the driver's side of the vehicle. He wrenched open the back door and buckled Olivia inside, then climbed behind the wheel. "Ana's going to be okay. She's a federal agent, remember? She's trained for this."

Whether he'd meant the words for his daughter or for himself, he didn't know.

A final gunshot echoed off the mountains, and he slowed his reach for the glove compartment. Ana. His heart threatened to beat straight out of his chest as the seconds ticked by. Maybe a full minute. No other shots registered. Did that mean—

Movement shifted in the rearview mirror.

"Get down!" He spun in his seat a split second before a bullet cracked the front windshield. Olivia's scream spurred Benning into action. He reached for the keys in the glove box, hit the remote start, and shoved the vehicle into Drive. Snow kicked up behind them, blocking his view of the shooter as they fishtailed onto the main road. Leaving the cabin, the deadline and Ana behind.

FLAKES FELL IN even sheets as Agent Evan Duran followed the fast-vanishing trail of footprints around the back of the property. The TCD safe house had been compromised by a single shooter determined to get his hands on the skull Benning Reeves had recovered from a Britland Construction property. Only now the evidence was missing. Along with Ramirez.

"What the hell happened here?" JC Cantrell straightened from a crouch beneath the shattered window on the north side of the house.

"I have no idea." Snow had been falling for the past few hours—long before he and Cantrell had tracked Ramirez's SUV and recovered Benning Reeves and his daughter on the shoulder of the 441— but failed to hide the stark pool of blood stained into the white backdrop. *Mierda*. Whether it'd come from the attacker or Ramirez, he didn't know, but whoever they were, they didn't have much time after losing that much blood. Whatever'd occurred here, Benning and Olivia Reeves were obviously lucky to be alive, even if that man had walked away with a fresh bullet in his shoulder. "I count three sets of adult footprints, one child. All of them coming from the back of the house."

"Let's move." JC withdrew his service weapon and raised it shoulder level. "If that blood belongs to Ramirez, we might already be too late."

In the year Agent Ramirez had joined Tactical Crime Division, there wasn't a lot she'd revealed to the team about her past. She'd transferred from missing persons, but other than that, she liked to keep to herself, which he respected. Every agent on their team had secrets. The TCD worked together, trusted each other with their lives when it counted, but that didn't mean they had to give up their entire personal histories. He imagined Ana Sofia Ramirez had one hell of a story to tell. Evan had noted the way she isolated herself from the rest of the team, insisted on them calling her by her last name, how she took on every case with a detachment he usually only saw in veteran agents who'd seen too much over the years. There was a reason behind it, a familiarity.

She'd lost someone close to her—violently—and in that regard, he and Ramirez were probably more alike than she realized. If it hadn't been for Annalise, he never would've seen past all that anger, that pain that came with losing the person he cared about to circumstances he couldn't control. Even worse, the guilt that if he'd only been strong enough, fast enough, he could've stopped it from happening in the first place. No matter how old he'd been at the time when his sister was taken.

Ramirez carried that same guilt now and had been investing it into saving as many lives as she could as though she was searching for some kind of redemption. He didn't know for whom, didn't have to, but it wasn't any way to live. The Tactical Crime Division had been created for rapid response, but even then, it was impossible to save everyone. As long as Ramirez refused to accept that, she'd destroy everything and everyone she cared about in the process. Then again, she had to have survived whatever had happened here to get that chance. Evan tapped JC on the shoulder twice. "On your six."

Unholstering his own weapon, he pressed his shoulders against the exterior of the cabin and put one foot in front of the other until they reached the corner. He waited until JC cleared them to move and followed close on his partner's heels. His heart pounded loud behind his ears as they neared the large pile of wood straight ahead. Countless bullet casings peppered the snow, more blood. Someone had taken cover behind the wall of wood, and another... He traced the path of footsteps near the tree line. And caught sight of a body twenty feet ahead. "JC."

"I see it." They moved as one, ready for anything in case whoever'd ambushed the safe house hadn't gotten far. Wouldn't be the first time a killer had stuck around to soak up the aftermath of what they'd done. Weapons raised, both agents searched the area for signs of movement as they closed the distance between them and the unidentified victim. The remains burned to a crisp in the fireplace on Benning Reeves's property, the charm linking back to one of Ramirez's old cases, now this. The bodies were piling up, too fast to keep up with.

JC crouched beside the body, rolling the victim onto their side. Long, dark hair spilled away from a familiar face, and dread fisted a tight knot in Evan's stomach. Blood drenched the front of her body from what looked like two bullet wounds—one in her side and one above her right breast—and a wound that'd obviously been a rushed patch job in the field in her left thigh. How she'd survived long enough to ensure Benning Reeves and his daughter had escaped, he didn't know, but they sure as hell owed her their lives. "Ramirez. *Hijo de*—"

"She's alive. I've got a pulse, but barely." Pulling his bare hand from her neck, JC holstered his weapon, then ripped her coat down the middle. "We can't move her like this, and it'll take two hours before EMTs can get here by road."

In a single breath Evan had his phone in his hand and pressed to his ear. The line connected directly to Director Jill Pembrook's private cell almost instantly. A gust of frigid air worked under Evan's jacket as JC stared up at him, his partner's expression blank, helpless. They didn't have a lot of time. Not if they were going to save Ramirez's life. The line connected. "I need a chopper to the Sevierville safe house now." He studied the lack of color in Ramirez's face, then let his attention drift lower to her injuries. "We've got an agent down."

Chapter Nine

Numb.

She couldn't feel her fingers, toes, or anything in between, but the soft beeping from nearby said she wasn't dead. If she was, heaven sucked. Ana struggled to open her eyes. Dim fluorescent lighting, scratchy sheets, uncomfortable bed with a remote next to her hand. Hospital. But the weight pressing into her left side didn't fall in line with previous experiences she'd had in places like this. Raising her head, she stiffened as her chin collided with a head of soft, beautiful auburn hair.

"She didn't want you to have to wake up alone." That voice. His voice. The IV in her hand ensured she couldn't physically feel the pain her body was in, but she still felt the tug of her insides when he spoke. Bright blue eyes steadied on her, and everything that'd happened since he'd inserted himself back into her life vanished. Leaving only him, leaving Olivia.

"You weren't…supposed to come back for me."

Her mouth tasted dry, bitter. How long had she been here? Hours? Days?

"That credit goes to your team. Agents Cantrell and Duran tracked the SUV's location after I called them from a burner phone you'd left in the glove compartment." He rested his elbow on his knees, one hand intertwined with hers. Shadows darkened under his eyes, his voice choked by something she couldn't put her finger on. "I wasn't going to leave you there to die, Ana. Not after everything you've done for us."

Was that why he was here? Because she'd done her job and he thought he owed her some semblance of repayment? Pain worked through her chest as she tried to sit higher in the bed, but the morphine dripping from the clear bag above her head should've taken care of that. No. This pain was something she hadn't allowed herself to feel for a long time. She'd spent so long trying to control her feelings, trying not to let people get close. While she and Benning had reunited after all these years in grief, held together by blood and fear, facing down the man who could've taken it all away had brought one life-altering realization into focus: moving on to the next case would hurt far more than ever before. In a matter of days, he and the precious soul tucked into Ana's side had carved their way into her heart without her realizing it until it was too late. Leaving would take everything she had left.

"How is she?" Ana set her mouth at the crown

of Olivia's head and inhaled the scent of shampoo. Memories flashed like lightning across her mind. She'd provided cover for Benning and Olivia as they'd raced through the trees toward the SUV. Only…she'd taken another bullet before they'd reached the vehicle. She'd tried to stay on her feet, tried to give them a chance, but she'd lost too much blood and her body hadn't been able to take any more. She'd collapsed. The man in the mask had stood over her, weapon aimed directly at her head, but then…she'd blacked out.

"She's fine. Thanks to you. We made it to the SUV and were able to get out of there before he could get to us." Benning rubbed circles into the pressure point between her index finger and thumb, and an immediate sense of calm flooded through her. "You saved our lives, Ana, and I'll never be able to repay you for that, but don't ever do that again. We almost lost you."

Air caught in her throat. The way he'd said those last four words almost made her believe his concern was more than professional courtesy, and her insides warmed. Did that mean… No. He might've been right about the fact her guilt had colored her relationships with the people around her, but she wasn't stupid enough to believe that any feelings built from their stress-induced situation were real. Or would last. She couldn't give in to that hope. Not when she still had so much work to do. Smoothing Olivia's hair out of her face, she rested her cheek on top of the girl's head. "I gave you my word. I'm not going anywhere. Not until I find your son."

The blue of his eyes deepened in color. Sliding his hand from around hers, he leaned back in his chair and ran his uninjured hand through his hair. "They lost the shooter's trail about a quarter mile into the woods. He must've had an ATV or a snowmobile waiting. He'd planned everything before he'd even walked into that cabin. And without him, I don't know if I'll ever see my son again." He picked up the phone she'd taken from the shooter, the one loaded with video of Owen. Alone, in the dark. The hospital staff must've recovered it with her personal effects when she'd been brought in, but seeing Benning with it pooled dread at the base of her skull. "Except with this."

"How many times have you watched that?" she asked.

"I lost count after they brought you out of surgery." He smoothed the pad of his thumb across the screen, and, even though she couldn't see the video clearly, she had the feeling he was imagining smoothing his son's face. "Your team is still processing my house, and they won't let me go inside, so this is all I have of him right now. A video."

"Benning, you have every reason to hate me right now for turning down that bastard's offer, but I promise you, he was never going to give up Owen's location. He would've baited you until you were no longer useful, then killed you both, and I couldn't let that happen." She wanted to reach out for him, take the phone from him, protect him from the pain so obviously pushing him to his breaking point. And protect herself from feeling that same pain.

"I don't hate you." His words barely registered over the beeping of the monitors at her side. "I tried. Those first few weeks after I'd found out you'd requested to be transferred back to Washington, I was angry. At first, I didn't understand what I could've said or if I'd done something wrong." His gaze narrowed on her, head cocked to the side. "But no matter how many times I tried to move on, even after I married Lilly, had the twins, lost her, you were still in the back of my mind. I hated myself more for not being strong enough to realize you weren't coming back than I ever hated you. Now you're the only one standing between my family and the man who wants us dead."

"I'm sorry." She didn't know what else to say but understood those two words couldn't possibly make up for the months—years—of raw pain Benning had endured. She rolled her lips between her teeth and bit down, but the morphine made it hard for her to know how much pressure was too much, and after a few seconds, she tasted salt in her mouth. A small price to pay for what she'd left behind. "It sounds grim, but the shooter still has the leverage to use your son in order to recover the skull. I know it doesn't seem like it, but we still have a chance to bring Owen home."

"No, we don't." His humorless laugh tugged at

something deep inside. He sat fully back in his chair, shadows deepening the exhaustion etched into his expression. He studied the phone in his hand one more time before setting it facedown on the end table beside her bed. "I don't know where the damn thing is."

"What do you mean?" She tried to sit up in the bed, but Olivia's weight pinned her to the mattress, and her strength wasn't what it used to be before taking two bullets and having her leg punctured by a window. "You told me—"

"That I hid it inside that fireplace where your team found Jo's body, and I did," he said. "But they didn't recover it, the killer doesn't have it and I'm not the one who moved it."

The scorched remains belonged to Benning's nanny? Her heart sank as she studied the bandage taped over her broken trigger finger. So much blood, so many innocent lives just…gone. It was her job to protect the innocent and find the guilty, but she couldn't even stomach looking at the damage to the rest of her body. Not without reminding herself of who'd she'd almost lost in the span of a few hours. How much more she would've lost if it hadn't been for him. Raising her gaze to his, she tried to clear her head of him, of his daughter pressed against her side, of all the distractions that could get in the way in finding the scared little boy in that video. But over the course of this investigation, Benning Reeves had made it very hard for her to stay numb.

Owen and Olivia's abductor had returned to the scene to clean up his mess, but he hadn't found what he'd killed an innocent woman over. If Ana had been able to physically feel anything in that moment, she would've had a headache pounding behind her ears. This didn't make sense. Someone else had gotten to the evidence before they could, but that still left the question of how Owen's kidnapping connected to the Samantha Perry case. It wasn't a coincidence that the charm had showed up at the scene of a body dump, and it wasn't a coincidence the shooter had blamed her for that girl's death. There had to be something linking the two investigations. Something she wasn't seeing. "Who else knew about the skull?"

"Nobody." Benning shook his head, that dark, shoulder-length hair stark against his white long-sleeved shirt. He'd showered, changed, but the shadows under his eyes said he hadn't rested during the time she'd been recovering. He'd stayed. Maybe at his daughter's insistence, but still, it meant a lot. More than it probably should have. There weren't a whole lot of people in her life that would've done the same.

"I need to brief my team." The dim lighting was suddenly too bright then, her body aching more with each passing second. The key piece of evidence in this case was missing, Owen Reeves was still out there and the shooter had nearly killed them all in the process. Ana sat up, ripping the IV from her hand, and Benning shot to his feet.

"What are you doing?" He peeled Olivia from her side.

Infierno, her body hurt, but Ana couldn't just sit here. The SOB shouldn't have been able to find them. Not unless he'd hacked into her vehicle's GPS system, which meant her entire team was officially at risk. "The shooter knew where to find us. I want to know how."

SOMETIMES THE AIR stilled before the onset of a hurricane.

Ana hadn't said a word since her discharge from the hospital, but he had no doubt in his mind that her silence wasn't a sign of weakness or pain. She'd survived two bullet wounds and a nick to her femoral artery from being shoved out a second-story window. If anything, the intensity in which she studied what had been left of his house, the way she curled her uninjured hand into a fist, could be seen as the calm before the storm. Because he wasn't sure there was anything that could bring her down.

Olivia barreled past both of them on her way toward the hallway leading to the back bedrooms. "Ana, come see my room!"

The woman at his side let a laugh escape past her lips, and Benning held on to that sound for as long as he could, committed it to memory. He didn't think he'd hear it again after what'd gone down at the safe house, but it was good to know it was still there. Buried, but there. "Thank you. For letting me stay here. I know it's not ideal, having to come back here after everything that's happened, but I'll make sure you get reimbursed for any damage the crime scene techs or my team might've caused."

"I don't care about any of that. What matters is that you have a place to recover while we figure the rest of this out. I think it'll be good for Olivia, too. Being somewhere familiar." He tried to ignore the fact all his furniture had been moved or that the rug his mother had woven by hand before he'd been born had disappeared from the living room. The property, including the house his father had built with his own two hands, had been left to him by his parents when they'd passed a few years ago. It'd always felt like home, a sanctuary where he and the kids could let go at the end of the day, stay away from the fast-paced, ever-growing city. A place he could build a family. Only now it felt…cold. Empty. Like something was missing.

Benning cleared his throat. Hiking her duffel into his good hand, he nodded down the hall. "You're welcome to take my room. It's not much, but you won't have to sleep on a twin-size bed that may or may not have cookie crumbs in the sheets." Benning shifted his weight between both feet as a smile pulled at the edges of his mouth. "Owen doesn't think I know he gets up in the middle of the night to steal cookies out of the pantry. He's not very quiet, for one, and he usually has a chocolate mustache in the morning."

"Has problems with authority, huh? Good luck

with that." Her gaze met his, and the smile relaxed as his own words settled between them. Something *was* missing, and it had been since the night he'd been knocked unconscious on this very floor. Hints of her sultry scent filled the space between them as she faced him, her hand grazing his arm. Bruising darkened the thin skin along the column of her throat as she stared up at him, and he rested his uninjured hand against the markings. Her pulse raced under his touch, and he couldn't help but revel in the knowledge he'd done that to her. He'd affected her, just as she affected him. "Benning, you don't have to do this until you're ready. We can get a couple rooms in town or find another safe house—"

He lowered his mouth to hers.

Hell, she was so damn perfect, so damn strong. She stood there as though everything that'd occurred hadn't fazed her when his entire world had been ripped apart. She was everything he needed right now—his anchor, his confidante, his motivation to keep going—and he'd almost lost her. Again. Only this time had been different. This time he'd truly believed he'd never see her again, and that knowledge, combined with Olivia's pleas to turn the SUV around, nearly had him putting his daughter's life at risk to go back for her. Her hand latched on to his arm as though she'd needed him as much as he'd been craving her, and he brought her fully against his body. Desire burned through him as she rose on her toes best as she could to get that much closer. His uninjured hand gripped her waist as he maneuvered her backward toward the hallway. "End of the hall."

Her exhales mingled with his as she nodded confirmation.

The Tactical Crime Division was still running background checks on Britland Construction employees, trying to find a weakness that would lead them to a suspect in this case. Confirming his nanny had been the victim recovered from the fireplace and the discovery of the charm that might have significance to the Samantha Perry case, solidified his hunger for the woman in his arms. With all the chaos and fear spreading around them, this was what they needed. A chance to block it all out, to escape. To remember. There was nothing left for them to do tonight. Nothing that could keep them apart, and for the first time in seven years, he'd have exactly what he—

"What are you doing?" a familiar voice asked.

Benning jumped as he realized his daughter had been standing less than a foot away, his heart jerking in his chest. He fought to control his breathing as he stepped back from Ana. Running a hand through his hair, he tried to put a lid on the heat exploding from behind his sternum, but it was no use. He'd never been able to control himself when it came to Ana Sofia Ramirez. "What have I told you about sneaking up on people?"

Bright blue eyes that matched his own shifted

from him to Ana and back. "How am I supposed to be a private investigator if I don't sneak?"

Ana's laugh raised his awareness of her all the more. She tried to hide the tint of red climbing from her neck into her cheeks with one hand, and he couldn't help but feel a bit of that embarrassment. "She has a good point."

"I thought you were supposed to be in bed." Crouching, he wrapped Olivia in a one-armed hug and tried not to think about the fact he'd nearly undressed the federal agent assigned to protect them without knowing his daughter had been in the room.

"I want to have a sleepover in your room," Olivia said.

"Baby, Ana is going to sleep in my room tonight, and I'm going to be in Owen's room." At least, that was the plan now. Benning raised his gaze to Ana as she gave them some space as though she didn't want any part of the conversation. He hadn't exactly been dedicated to the idea of filling the hole Owen and Olivia's mother had left behind when she'd died, but Ana was as much part of this family as his wife had ever been now. Maybe even more so considering what'd happened over the past three days.

"No, that's okay." Ana reached for her duffel bag, pain filling her expression as she hauled it to her side. "You guys can take the big bed, and I can sleep in Olivia's room. I'll be fine."

"We should all sleep over in Daddy's bed!" An exaggerated gasp filled the living room. Excitement lit Olivia's features as she bounced in his arms. A brightness he hadn't seen in days filled her eyes, and he couldn't help but enjoy the effect. Three days. Her twin brother, the person she'd never lived a single day of her life without, had been missing for three days. Benning would take all the smiles and jumping he could get out of her.

Then he realized what she was asking. "Honey, I'm sure Ana wants her own bed. You remember she got hurt fighting off that bad man? She needs her rest, and you have a lot of energy when you're sleeping."

"But I want to have a sleepover with Ana." In an instant his daughter—the master of manipulation—wiped the excitement from her features. Tears welled in her eyes, and everything inside him surrendered.

Benning relaxed his chin toward his chest, pulling on the bullet wound in his shoulder. "You've got to be kidding me."

"Uh, yeah. We could do that. It'll be fun," Ana said.

He snapped his head up. "What?"

Ana's attention bounced between him and Olivia as she motioned to his daughter's unicorn pajamas. "It's just… I don't have anything to wear."

"I have something! It was my mom's! I'll go get it." Olivia raced through the kitchen toward the other side of her house to her room, the tears gone in an instant.

"It's a sleepshirt I kept of Lilly's after she died. I

thought Olivia might want to wear it when she was big enough. You know, just something she could have of her mom's." Benning straightened. What was happening? He was the one who was supposed to be sleeping over with Ana. Not the three of them in the same bed. "But you don't have to wear it, and you don't have to let her guilt you into a sleepover. She denies it flat out, but she kicks in the middle of the night. Hard."

Hesitation tensed her shoulders.

"Benning, I don't want to insert myself somewhere I shouldn't. I'm not her mom, and we're... We're not together anymore. So if you think this is a bad idea, I can take her twin-size bed or find a hotel room for the night." Ana swiped her tongue between her lips, homing his attention to her mouth, and every nerve ending he owned fired in response. "But I'm not going to lie, that girl is hard to say no to."

"I should've warned you, she's a professional manipulator." He slid his hand into hers. "Lilly and I had an arrangement after we found out she was pregnant with the twins. We would raise our kids together to give them a stable home, love them, provide for them, but that was where our marriage ended. We were open to the possibility that, maybe, down the line there would be more between us, but it didn't work out that way, and Owen and Olivia have never known their mother. I can't say I didn't care for her at all. I did. Without her, I wouldn't have the two best humans I could've asked for, but I need to make one thing clear with you, Ana." He traced the tendons along her inner wrist, locking his gaze with hers. "I never stopped loving you."

Her mouth parted, her kiss-stung lips begging for his attention again.

Olivia raced into the room. "I found it!"

What was with this girl having the worst timing imaginable? Did she wait around corners for the chance to ambush him and Ana at every turn? Hell. His body wasn't going to be able to take this much longer.

"Great." Pulling her hand from his, Ana took the sleepshirt from his daughter and smiled. Her hand found its way into Olivia's as they all headed down the hallway toward his bedroom. Ana cast a glance over her shoulder toward him. "Looks like we're ready for that sleepover."

Chapter Ten

The sound of utensils scraping against glass plates pulled her back into reality.

Warm blankets had been piled around her, hints of pine and soap tickling her nose, but the rest of Benning's queen-size bed was empty. She'd fallen asleep at the edge, pressed right against the snoring six-year-old who'd worked past her defenses and straight into her heart. And the man on the other side? She could still feel the warmth of his hand sliding across hers against the headboard as Olivia slept between them. Minutes had gone by, maybe hours, as they'd drifted off to sleep, their gazes connected with one another in the dark, and she couldn't remember a time when she'd slept so well.

Her entire body ached, muscles she hadn't even known existed protesting as she slowly eased her legs over the side of the bed. The wound from the pane of glass in her thigh dulled to a low throb as she settled her toes into the plush rug perfectly centered around the bed. The space—Benning's room—was simple.

Wooden nightstands on either side of the bed, with lamps that looked like they'd come straight from the pile of firewood she could see out the window now. Framed pictures of the twins had been strategically placed so he had to see them first thing in the morning, no matter which side of the bed he rolled out of.

Ana couldn't help but pick up the one nearest her. Of Owen. He must've been two—maybe three— when the photo had been taken. He'd lifted his arms straight up in the air as though he'd made a touchdown from his position in the middle of the kitchen. Then she noticed the full-size carrots set on top of each of the cabinet drawer pulls, and she couldn't help but laugh. Pain rolled across her chest from the second bullet she'd taken, and she set her hand over the bandage. Blood soaked through the gauze, staining the sleepshirt Olivia had let her borrow. She carefully replaced the frame on the nightstand and used her uninjured leg for balance to stand. *"Maldicion."*

"One of these days you're going to have to translate all the swear words you say when you think nobody is listening." His voice coiled through her, reaching past the aches and pains, deep into the self-doubt and fear that'd plagued her since she'd taken on this case.

"I got blood on Lilly's shirt." She faced him, nearly knocked back by the primal attraction heating her veins as she looked at him. He leaned against the door frame, muscled arms crossed over his chest, and for a split second, she couldn't remember what she'd been so upset about. He'd changed his clothes, kept his hair damp from his most recent shower and brought her a plate of something that smelled so good her stomach lurched. *Infierno,* he was a god among mere mortals. And she'd been stupid enough to walk away from him. "I'm sorry. I'll wash it before Olivia notices."

"Honestly, she'll probably love it even more now." He moved into the room, hints of the scent she'd caught from the sheets intensifying tenfold, and she couldn't get enough. Of him. Of this place. Of the smiling faces in the picture frames set around the room. It was everything she hadn't realized she'd wanted until now as he pinned her with that bright blue gaze. He stepped closer, offering the plate. "Thought you might be hungry."

"Thank you." Awareness of how very little clothing she'd gone to sleep in warmed her straight through. The T-shirt and pair of his oversize sweats were enough to keep her warm when Olivia had stolen the blankets in the middle of the night but felt like nothing when he studied her from head to toe as he did now. She took the plate from him, her body tingling with the unrequited desire that'd shot down her spine last night before Olivia had caught them kissing. She tried focusing on the plate in her hand and not the fact they were seemingly out of range of his daughter. Eggs, waffles and bacon warmed her palm through the plate. Her favorites. Had that been on purpose? "But I should tell you my team hasn't been able to link any of Britland Construction's employees to this case, or the charm they recovered from your property. Whoever has Owen could've just taken advantage of an opportunity to hide the skull on that site. Official access be damned. I have my team looking for the rest of it. Hopefully, we can find something that will give us an ID in case the skull is never recovered."

"They couldn't match ballistics from the bullet casings they recovered at the safe house, either." Her gaze snapped to his. Pressure built behind her sternum the longer he invaded her personal space— that rich, addictive scent of his filling her lungs. He cocked his head to one side, a playful smile tugging at one corner of his mouth. A mouth she'd kissed less than twelve hours ago, a mouth she wanted more of now. Her gaze dropped to his lips in memory. No matter what happened at the end of this investigation, she'd remember that kiss. Remember him. "Agent Cantrell stopped by to fill me in this morning while you were still sleeping. I didn't tell him you'd spent the night in my bed fighting a six-year-old for a corner of the mattress."

A laugh escaped her chest, and she flinched against the ache, sliding her hand over the wound. She set the plate on the end of the bed to avoid dropping it at her feet. "Don't make me laugh. It hurts too much."

"Here." Benning helped her down onto the bed with his uninjured hand, then disappeared into the bathroom for two breaths before reappearing with a bottle of rubbing alcohol, medical tape and fresh gauze in hand. "We should change your bandage."

"Already prepared," she said. "Were you expecting I'd get shot?"

"I live with two sociopaths who don't learn their lessons about running through the house with sharp objects." Setting everything across the end of the bed one-handed, he crouched in front of her, his gaze level with her chest. Callused fingers made quick work of pulling the collar of her shirt lower, removing the bandage over her stitches and cleaning both fresh and crusted blood from the area. Every move he made, every swipe of his fingers against her skin, hiked her heart rate into overdrive. All she had to do was reach out and touch him…and she'd have everything she'd ever wanted. "I can't tell you how many times I had to clean the gash on Owen's head after he ran into the brick fireplace because he wouldn't leave the damn thing alone."

She hissed as the cotton swab he was using pulled at her stitches, and stinging pain slipped past her constant hold on her reactions.

"Sorry," he said. "I've got to clean it all or it might get infected."

"It's fine." She wanted to turn away, to hide the fact she wasn't completely under control at that moment from him, but there was nowhere for her to run. She wanted to be the woman who'd stopped at nothing to protect him and his children from harm for him, who'd stared down a killer without blinking, but the numbness and mental distance had started to fade. He'd gotten beneath her skin, lit the darkest parts of herself she'd kept hidden from everyone around her, and she was starting to lose the battle. Physically. Mentally. Emotionally. Locking her teeth together, she released the breath she'd been holding as the stinging dulled and studied his work. "You're pretty good at this."

"Well, you're pretty good at getting yourself shot." He trailed his hands to the bandage strapped across her upper thigh, igniting a path of heat and goose bumps. "And stabbed. Like I said, I've had a lot of practice."

"Hey, let's get one thing straight, okay? The window stabbed me, and that was not my fault." His smile melted the remaining tension down her spine and fisted tight around her heart. Always the giver, always looking out for someone else. That was the kind of man he was. Caring, considerate. She didn't deserve him. "Would you change any of it? The calls from school, the trips to the emergency room, sweeping cookie crumbs out of sheets on a daily basis."

"Not a thing." Peeling back the tape from the wound in her thigh, he changed out the dressing quickly, but his hand didn't fall away when he was finished. In an instant a rush of sensation fired through her. There was a breath, one moment, where her fear released its hold on her, and she leaned in to finish what they'd started last night.

"Daddy?" Olivia asked from the door.

"Damn it, I really need to put a bell on that girl." Benning ducked his head, his hand sliding from her thigh, and he turned toward his daughter standing in the door frame. "What is it, baby? Are you still hungry?"

"I miss Owen." Sunlight streamed through the windows centered over each nightstand beside the bed, highlighting the well of tears in the girl's eyes, and something inside Ana broke. Something she hadn't let herself feel since realizing her baby sister wasn't going to be coming home. No matter how many times Ana and her brothers had searched, they'd had to accept their sister was gone. "Can he come home now, Daddy? Please?"

In three steps Benning had his daughter wrapped in his big arms, her face buried in his shoulder as he stroked her hair. "Everything is going to be okay, Liv. Owen is going to be home soon. I promise. We're working with Ana's team to find him, and he'll be annoying the heck out of you sooner than you think."

Turning her attention to getting dressed, Ana was aware the moment wasn't meant for her. No matter how easy it'd been to fall back into old habits, familiarities and jokes, she wasn't part of this family. And she never would be. The work she did couldn't be compromised. Not by her past experiences. Not by the six-year-old girl who'd wrapped her arms around Ana as she'd gone to sleep last night, and definitely not by the man determined to take up too much space in her head.

"Will the skull you put in the fireplace help find him faster?" Olivia asked.

Ana twisted around, her heart in her throat. "What'd you say?"

Maneuvering Olivia back at arm's length, Benning wiped his daughter's tears with the pads of his thumbs, then gripped both her arms. He lowered his voice. "Olivia Kay Reeves, tell me you aren't the one who took that skull from the fireplace."

"I wanted to solve the case." Olivia's face fell as another round of tears streaked down her flawless cheeks. "I brought it to my lab."

"What lab?" Ana took a single step forward.

Benning slid his hands down his daughter's arms as he turned to face Ana. "She and Owen built a fort in the backyard where they like to pretend to solve cases. The skull must be there."

"She really is one hell of an agent," Ana said.

"I wish that made me feel better." All this time the evidence he'd removed from Britland's construction site had been right in his own backyard. Well, it'd been in his backyard before, but his daughter wasn't supposed to be the one who'd found it. His stomach knotted. This was the kind of thing nightmares were made of, and Olivia had... Hell, she'd done what any good investigator would've done and preserved the evidence. "Six-year-olds aren't supposed to hide bones from their parents in a fort in their backyard."

The forensic techs pulled the evidence from the makeshift fort his kids had built out of extra two-by-fours and subfloor from one of the sites he'd inspected last summer. Owen and Olivia had spent every waking second in their hideout when the weather was good. In fact, he'd had to drag them into the house by their ears for dinner on many occasions. Now it was a crime scene, stained by the very thing he was trying to protect them from.

"We have the skull now. My team will run DNA and dental records, and we'll figure out time and cause of death." Ana slipped her hands into her jacket pockets. "If Olivia hadn't moved it, the killer would've gotten ahold of it first and destroyed the evidence, Benning. Getting an ID on this victim is how we get your son back."

She was right, but at what point would it be okay to say his family had been through enough? How much more blood, fear and near-death experiences did he and his kids have to take before what he'd built cracked beyond repair? Olivia could obsess over becoming an investigator all she wanted, but there was a difference between reading about this kind of stuff in her mystery novels and seeing it firsthand, and he didn't want any part of it. Not for her. Not for the woman at his side. What kind of life was that? What kind of person wasn't affected by this kind of work on a deep, scarring level? Benning knew the answer the second the question had crossed his mind, and right then he understood. Understood the deeper reason why Ana had chosen to cut herself off from her family and friends…from him. Understood why she'd kept her emotions out of relationships, and how she was able to step onto scenes like this over and over again with a kind of numbness and detachment. Because without that boundary in place, she risked the people she cared about the most. Nobody—not even she—could handle a lifetime of that kind of guilt if something happened to one of them. "How do you do it? All the pain, the death, the risk of endangering the people you care about. You've made a career out of stuff like this, and I can't even handle it for a few days."

One breath. Two.

"You know as well as I do it doesn't come without a cost, but I realized a long time ago giving people another chance to live their life is worth the sacrifice." Ana limped toward the scene, then paused, turning back toward him. Controlled chaos played out behind her, but the world seemed to disappear in the moment her eyes lifted to his. No crime scene techs, no body parts being collected and bagged in his backyard. It was just the two of them. Hints of red colored the tip of her nose and cheeks, the confidence in her eyes overwhelming. "You're stronger than you think you are, Benning. The only reason your kids are still here is because you fought to protect them.

Remember that the next time you ask yourself if you're doing enough. You're everything to them."

Yet, he'd been the one to put them in danger in the first place.

A car door slammed from the other side of the property, and he turned his attention to the older, white-haired couple headed for the front of the house. Lilly's parents.

Benning faced the elongated front porch he and his father had built a few years ago, studying Olivia with her notebook and pen in hand as she rocked back and forth in the hanging swing. He used to rock her and Owen to sleep as babies on it. It'd been the three of them, one of them in each arm, and the crickets on that swing when he'd promised to protect them for the rest of their lives. For the first time he could remember, he'd failed.

The brightness in Olivia's expression gripped his heart in a vise as he climbed the stairs and sat beside her. She was obviously having the time of her life watching real investigators and technicians collect evidence, taking notes on what they did, what they said, how they bagged the evidence. He swiped his uninjured hand down his face. She'd found a human skull in their fireplace and had moved it without hesitation to solve the crime herself. Hell, he had to start watching what kind of stuff she was reading. "Liv, I need you to go spend a couple nights with Grandma and Grandpa while I help the FBI look for your brother. It'll be safer for you there."

He and Lilly hadn't had the greatest relationship. Really, they'd only gotten married to make it easier on the kids as they got older, but he'd always liked and respected her parents, and they loved their grandchildren despite the choices he and Lilly had made. He trusted them to watch over and be there for his daughter in case…he couldn't. Benning bit the inside of his cheek to counter the sinking sensation in his stomach.

The scribbling on her note pad slowed. "I want to stay with you."

He moved a piece of long brown hair out of her face and tucked it behind her ear as his insides tore bit by bit. He should've gone straight to the police after he'd found the skull instead of coming home because Owen had been sick. Should've been strong enough to fight off the bastard who'd taken his kids. Should've gone after Ana seven years ago when he'd had the chance so there wasn't this invisible distance between them now. His life was full of wrong choices, but he'd never forgive himself if something happened to Olivia because of his own selfish need to keep her close. "I know, but think of it this way. Grandma has a whole bunch of mystery novels you haven't read yet."

Curiosity pulled her attention from the crime scene, and those beautiful blue eyes widened. "How many?"

"She told me she ordered a ton of new ones for you last week." He settled one elbow on his knee, leveling his shoulder with hers. Nudging her with his arm, he unbalanced her enough to keep her attention on him. "Thirty. Maybe more."

"And I get to read them all?" she asked.

"I told Grandma you get to read as many of them as you want." Threading his hand in hers, he helped her off the swing and nodded toward Lilly's parents. Within two minutes Olivia, her booster seat and the bag he'd packed for her were loaded into the back of his in-laws' pickup truck. "I'm going to see you in a couple days, okay?"

"Okay." She hugged her bag tighter. "Don't forget to call me tonight when I go to bed."

"I will, baby. See you soon." He kissed the top of her head, memorized the way the scent of her shampoo tickled the back of his throat, then shut her inside and stepped back. Slush kicked up behind the pickup's tires as his daughter centered her face in the rear window and stared back at him with a small wave. He waved back, and something inside him cracked. First, Owen had been taken from him. Now he needed Olivia as far from this case as possible.

"You made the right decision." Ana stepped into his side, her soft, dark hair lifting into his face as wind ripped through the trees, and a shiver raced down his spine. She'd been there nearly every step of the way, protected his daughter from harm, nearly died to ensure he and Olivia had made it to safety at the cabin, and was working tirelessly to locate his son. Where his heart threatened to shred in his chest as his in-laws turned onto the main road back toward Sevierville, Ana was there trying to hold him together. She'd always been there. Because he hadn't been able to let her go all this time.

"There was nothing to think about. Every second she's around me is another chance that bastard can get his hands on her." Warmth spread down his arm as she curled her fingers around his inner elbow. "I should've gotten her out of town when I had the chance, but I couldn't..."

"Stand the thought of losing her, too? I might know a little something about that." She did. More than he ever would. She buried her nose beneath the high collar of her jacket, then tucked her hands into her pockets, taking the heat she'd generated with her. "I could tell you it gets easier over time to help you feel better, but it'd be a lie."

"Has anyone ever told you your bedside manner could use some work?" he asked.

"I don't think anyone but you would have the guts." Her laugh pierced through the unsettling haze closing in on his thoughts as the pickup dipped below the horizon, and hell, he loved that sound. Loved the way her smile reached her eyes, how her smile lines perfectly framed her full lips, loved the way that laugh shot heat straight through his system. She nodded back over her shoulder toward the house. "Come on. It'll be a few hours before forensics has any information on the skull. Until then, we can make up for the sleep your daughter stole from us last night as soon as the tech team is finished. Then we can review the list of Britland Construction employees together. Make sure there's not someone on that list we need to take a closer look at."

The gut-wrenching weight of sending Olivia to his in-laws' farm for a couple days started to lift. How was it possible, in the most terrifying circumstances he'd ever imagined, Ana still kept him grounded, kept him from losing control? If he hadn't requested her to work this case, would he have been able to keep it together this long? Would the killer have gotten exactly what he'd wanted, and taken Benning and his twins down with him? The answer was already there, already cemented in reality. Without Ana, he would've lost everything. "I warned you what would happen if you agreed to a sleepover. You knew the risks going in, Agent Ramirez."

"Like I said, it's hard to say no to her," she said.

Benning slipped his hand into hers as she struggled to retrace her steps through the snow on her injured leg, and in that moment he found himself never wanting to let go. "Wait until she asks you to let her drive your SUV."

Chapter Eleven

This whole investigation would be easier if the evidence spelled out who'd taken Owen Reeves from this very house. Ana studied the official crime scene photos taken of the charm JC had recovered from Jo West's body disposal site. She and Benning had stayed up most of the night reviewing the employee list from Britland Construction, but none of the names—no matter how many times she'd read them—had jumped out at either of them. No criminal charges other than a few speeding tickets, no massive amounts of debt or visible connection to the Samantha Perry case either of them could see. From the outside it looked as though Britland Construction hired the best and most trustworthy assets despite the negligence Benning had uncovered and the skull he'd pulled from one of their project walls.

She'd gone over the interviews she and her partner had conducted seven years ago during the Samantha Perry case, searching the transcripts, rereading the file over and over until the words had started blurring together. Director Pembrook confirmed Samantha's best friend, Claire Winston, was currently serving her country in Afghanistan with her military unit and still wore the bracelet the friends had exchanged in high school while she was off duty. The charm had to belong to the teenage girl Ana hadn't been able to save, the one whose case had changed everything. It had to. It was too much of a coincidence for it to be random.

"There has to be something here." She fought to keep her eyes open, her entire body giving in to the exhaustion she'd been ignoring for the past three days. But she couldn't sleep. The kidnapper's twenty-four-hour deadline had expired. They should've uncovered a lead by now. Should've heard from the *bastardo* who'd taken Benning's son. But there'd been nothing. Tears burned in her eyes as defeat clawed through her. The all-too-familiar sinking sensation she'd worked hard to bury since she'd requested a transfer to Washington broke through her defenses. She had to find Owen, needed to find the boy who'd topped each of these cabinet pulls with carrots in that photo next to his father's bed. Because if she couldn't do this… If she couldn't bring that little boy home, it would destroy the man who'd worked past her defenses and given her a glance at what real happiness could look like. And she'd lose him all over again.

The thought sparked a chain reaction of disbelief and rage. She stilled, but her heart raced out of control. Three days. That was all it'd taken for

Benning to put her right back in the same position she'd been in when she'd received the call that Samantha Perry's body had been recovered. She'd become emotionally involved. Attached. Blind to the evidence right in front of her. She'd broken her own rule to keep her distance and fallen in love with the idea she wouldn't have to leave. But if she couldn't find Owen, his small, perfect family would be the ones who paid the price.

She shoved the stack of papers off the kitchen island with every ounce of anger and frustration and disappointment building inside, but spun too fast and stretched the stitches in her side. Pain spread fast, the air rushing out of her, and she had to catch herself before the gray wood-like tile throughout the kitchen rushed up to meet her. Bent over the bar stool, she clamped onto her side as the stinging dulled. She couldn't breathe, let alone think. "What have I done?"

Strong hands slid along her spine, and she twisted around to fight as his arms secured her against his muscled chest. No. She couldn't break. Not in front of him. The bullet wound beneath her collarbones protested as she pushed away from him, but he only held her tighter as the sobs broke past her control. Her knees threatened to give out, but he was there. Lending her his strength, letting her take what she needed from him. She fisted her unbroken fingers into his shirt as tremors racked through her. "What am I missing?"

Benning stared down at her, not an ounce of blame or hatred in his expression, only sympathy. And suddenly the agent she'd been fighting so hard to become shattered into a thousand pieces right in the middle of his kitchen. The hurt, the loss, the grief, the anger she'd had to live with each and every day broke through. She felt it all—everything she'd been trying to hide over the years—in a matter of seconds until her body couldn't take it anymore. He'd been right before. Detaching herself from feeling anything for the people she cared about had been tearing her apart, and she didn't know how to fix it. The tears streaked down her face as the truth she'd been holding on to for so long bubbled to the surface. "I couldn't save them. My sister, Samantha. I...failed."

"But you did everything you could, Ana, and that's what matters." He bent at the knees, scooping her into his arms, and it was then she'd noticed he wasn't wearing his arm sling. He was at risk of doing more damage to his shoulder, but he kept his attention focused on her. Always on her. The main level of his house passed in a blur as he carried her down the hall and into his bedroom. Laying her in his bed, his hands trailed to her boots, and he unlaced each one before discarding them onto the floor. Slowly, carefully. Treating her as though she were glass. Had anyone taken such care with her before? The mattress dipped as he took position beside her, his gaze centered on her. "You've been so focused on saving everybody else. But who's going to be there for you when you need it?"

She didn't know what to say, what to think. The

Tactical Crime Division—JC, Evan, Smitty, Davis, all of them—had become a large part of her life over the past year since Director Pembrook had requested her reassignment from missing persons, but there were still pieces of her she kept hidden from her team. From everyone. Her parents, her three brothers, the friends she'd cut from her life. Any one of them would race to help if she asked, but she didn't deserve their support. Not after what she'd done. He traced her jawline with callused fingers, and right then she couldn't escape the feeling he might know her better than she knew herself. In ways no one else had. "I…"

He leaned into her, pressing his mouth to her forehead as she slid her hand around his wrist, begging him not to leave. Closing her eyes, she reveled in his touch, in the way he always smelled of pine and outdoors, in how he made her feel wanted and strong and beautiful.

Trailing a path of soft kisses to her temple, then lower toward her ears, he brushed his beard against her oversensitized skin, and she shuddered. "Let me be that man who can be there for you, Ana. Tell me what you need. Don't think about it. Tell me what you need right now."

The answer sat on the tip of her tongue, but she didn't have the courage to say those words. Instead, she opened her eyes, framed his face between both hands and brought his mouth to hers. She kissed him hard, desperation sliding into every stroke of her tongue against his. She felt as if she'd been starving for air, and he was oxygen. He was her whole world in that moment, the only one who mattered. Her weaknesses, the lack of evidence, the night she'd walked away. None of it existed inside the bubble they'd created. Him. She needed him.

He leveraged his injured arm on the other side of her head, then latched on to her hip before his fingers moved beneath her shirt. Eyes—brighter than the clear blue sky—roamed down the length of her body, and every cell she owned heightened as though he'd physically touched her. "You are the strongest, most dedicated and beautiful woman I've ever known, and you deserve someone who's going to treat you like the queen you are, who will put your needs first and make you happy for the rest of your life."

"You make me happy." Her admission slipped past her lips without her permission, but she couldn't take it back now. She wouldn't. Because it was the truth. The three months they'd been together all those years ago had been the best of her life. Until now. These past few days, seeing him again, seeing him as a father to an amazing little girl and how dedicated he was to protect his children, had shifted something inside her. Opened up a lifetime of possibility she'd never considered before. Given her hope.

A slow smile stretched his lips thin. "You make me happy, too."

Carving a path through his beard with her fingernails, she lifted her mouth to his. What their mutual admission meant for the future, if they even had one,

Ana didn't know, but excitement coursed through her as she committed herself to finding out and chased back the fear burning through her. She'd spent her career dedicated to saving as many victims of violence as she could, put her entire life on hold to give them a chance to live the rest of theirs, but maybe she'd finally sacrificed enough to make up for her past. Maybe it was time for her to take that same chance she'd battled so hard to give to the victims who'd been taken. With him. With Owen and Olivia. "We have the house to ourselves now."

"Believe me, that's all I've been thinking about since we finished running through the Britland Construction employee directory." His voice graveled, warming her from the inside. He hauled her off the bed, careful of her injuries, and carried her into the attached bathroom. The same gray wood-like tile directed them toward a large open shower set at the farthest end of the space. Sharp layers of stone and rock made up the back wall of the shower, two square rainshower heads lighting up as Benning twisted on the water. In seconds he'd stripped himself, discarding his clothing outside the reach of the water pooling at their feet, and closed in on her. All predator. All hers. Ridges and valleys of muscle carved shadows across his abdomen, and her mouth watered. "I've been waiting for this moment for seven years."

Slowly pulling her shirt over her head to avoid the pain in her chest and shoulder, Ana gasped as he swept her under the shower spray with most of her clothes still on. A laugh escaped up her throat as she slid her now-wet hair out of her face. "You couldn't wait five more seconds?"

He kissed her again, his body pressed against the length of hers. "Not for you."

HE COULDN'T SLEEP, couldn't take his eyes off her, and after what they'd shared over the past three days, he knew why. He'd fallen in love with her all over again. This intelligent, confident, beautiful creature who'd slipped in and out of his life. But this time he wasn't going to let go. Chasing Olivia down with cookie dough at the safe house, sharing his bed with his daughter sandwiched between them, gasping his name as he'd memorized her body all over again in the privacy of the shower last night. It was as though she was already part of their lives, and, damn it, he didn't want to lose her again. Couldn't.

Long, dark eyelashes rested against her cheeks, but the change in her breathing patterns homed his attention to the light brown flawless skin of her neck and chest visible above the sheets. "I can feel you staring at me."

Pain filtered through his nerve endings and he realized he'd propped himself up on the wrong arm for a mere chance of seeing her clearly. "Does Quantico train all their agents in the art of having a sixth sense, or just you?"

"You don't need to flirt with me." Hazel-green eyes centered on his as her smile pierced straight through him. Leveraging her elbow into her pillow, mirroring him, she rested her head against her palm. And in that moment the woman he'd built in his head was more beautiful and mesmerizing than ever before. Exactly where she belonged. "You've already seduced me with your good looks."

"Is that all it takes?" He couldn't keep his laugh to himself, brushing one hand down his beard. "Damn. Wish I would've known that before now. Could've saved me a lot of time and frustration."

"Don't get me wrong, the free cookie crumbs in the sheets and the rainfall showerheads are a bonus." Skimming her hand across his chest, she shifted closer, her lips barely grazing his as she traced the muscled lines of his abdomen below the sheets. Instant desire seared through him, and he half expected his daughter to interrupt the moment, but the cabin remained silent. "I'm starting to wish we hadn't wasted so much time apart."

He closed his eyes. "Ana, I—"

Her phone vibrated from the nightstand, and she set her forehead against his chest. Reality penetrated through the haze they'd created since he'd witnessed her coming to terms with the past in the middle of his kitchen last night, and guilt ripped through him. He couldn't lie to himself. He'd needed the distraction from the case—from the anxiety he'd never find his son—as much as Ana had, and he wouldn't regret that, but they couldn't ignore their respective duties any longer. He needed to find his son, and she needed to find the SOB responsible for taking him. She reached for the phone before the device dipped off the edge of his nightstand, tapped the screen and brought it to her ear. "Ramirez."

Benning slipped from the bed, reaching for his clothes. He couldn't hear the voice on the other end of the line but imagined if there'd been news on his son's location, she'd get the message across.

"Are you sure?" The color drained from her face. Her attention drifted to him, and everything inside him tensed. Ana pinned her phone between her shoulder and ear as she rushed to get dressed. "I'm on my way. Have the director get in touch with Claire Winston again. I want her found. Now." Ana ended the call, and the hairs on the back of his neck stood on end. Something was happening. "That was Evan— Agent Duran. The forensic lab was working on identifying the owner of the skull, but when they went to compare dental records, they noticed something had been locked between the victim's teeth on the X-rays."

"Locked?" Intentionally or forced? Didn't matter. Whatever it was, it could lead them to the next step in this case, the next step to finding Owen. His throat dried as she bolted from the bed and started getting dressed. "What did they find?"

"A scales of justice charm. Exactly like the one we recovered from your property after Jo West's body was found in the fireplace." She slowed, facing him, her boots pinched in her grip. "So now we have two. One could belong to Samantha Perry and the other—"

"To her best friend. Claire Winston." Hell. Were they about to find another body? Benning sank onto the edge of the mattress, the past few hours evaporating as though they'd never happened. How many more people had to die before they were able to bring this bastard down? How many more had to suffer? "You want Claire found in case she's another victim. I thought your director confirmed she's serving with her unit in Afghanistan."

"As far as I know, that's the truth, but it wouldn't be hard to get someone to cover for her. And the army hasn't always been forthcoming about admitting one of their soldiers might be missing in action," she said.

"Why would she…" That didn't make sense. If Samantha Perry's best friend from high school had been targeted by the killer, how would she know she needed to lie about her whereabouts? Benning stood, his instincts screaming. "They got an ID on the skull, didn't they?"

"Yes." She tightened her broken hand around the phone but didn't even seem to notice the pain. "They were able to match both DNA from the bone marrow and dental records to Harold Wood."

Gravity cemented him in place. Samantha Perry's killer.

His mouth dried. "You think Claire might be involved in Owen's kidnapping?"

"I've seen people kill for much less than getting revenge for a best friend who never saw justice. Shoving a charm Samantha Perry wore up until her death in the mouth of her killer is personal. It's sending a message, and it's possible Claire is the one behind it." Ana's voice dropped, almost monotone, as the agent he'd gotten to know over the past few days surfaced. "But if Claire Winston is involved, she's not working alone. The attacker at the safe house was male. Trained, possibly former military. She'd have an extensive network of possible partners from her unit alone. All she'd have to do is convince one of them to help her get justice for Samantha."

"Claire killed Harold Wood and hid his body— or what was left of it—on the construction site, and I uncovered the evidence. She knew the charm and motive would link back to her if he was ever found." He pushed off the bed. Tension bled back into his shoulders and hands as the puzzle pieces started fitting together. "That's why my son has been kidnapped? So she wouldn't have to answer for the fact she killed her best friend's murderer?"

"We don't know that yet, Benning." She hauled the black duffel bag always within reach onto the bed, and dumped a box of bullets onto the sheets, and reloaded the magazine to her new service weapon. She was far more comfortable around a weapon than he was, and damn, he was thankful for it now. "We have to get to Claire's house. There might be something there we can use to prove she's involved, but we have to go now. The skull you pulled from the wall has been identified. Whoever took your son is going to try to make sure we can't connect his death back to them."

Benning studied how quickly she was able to assemble her weapon and holster it, even with a broken trigger finger wrapped in a brace and tape. The air crushed from his lungs as the realization hit. Hell, he loved her. He loved the strong, badass agent who'd protected him and his daughter from a killer, the vulnerable woman who couldn't forgive herself for her past failures. No matter how hard she tried to bury the side that made her more human, he loved her. Had never stopped loving her. He rounded to her side of the bed. "Ana, wait."

He'd told her the truth before. He'd tried hating her, tried focusing on making his marriage with Lilly work despite the fact neither of them were interested in anything more than being parents to the kids they'd created. But his heart had always had other ideas. Something deep down understood that what he felt in this moment was real, and certainty clicked into place. He wanted Ana Sofia Ramirez. Wanted her in his life, in his kids' lives, wanted her when times got hard, when she dropped her guard and especially when she tried to shut him out. He wanted every piece of her, and he didn't give a damn about how much it might hurt in the long run. Loving her would be easy. The rest of it? They'd just have to figure it out together. As a family. But he had to protect his kids at the same time.

"There's something I need to say to you first." His stomach flipped. Would she even want the responsibility of being with a man who had kids? She'd gotten along well enough with Olivia because his daughter was borderline obsessed with what Ana did for a living, but she'd never met Owen. Would the kids want her around, or would they see her as nothing more than a replacement for what they'd lost the day they were born? Would her job put Owen and Olivia at risk? Would she detach herself from them when a case went sideways as she'd done to him all those years ago? This sure as hell wasn't simple lust, but it was starting to turn more complicated all the same.

"Benning?" Ana maneuvered around the end of the bed, slowly closing the distance between them, and every nerve ending in his body went haywire. For her. Because of her. Handing him her backup weapon grip first, she stared up at him, concern etched into her expression.

"I want you to stay here after we recover Owen. With me," he said. "With us."

Her eyes widened, that legendary control failing her, and his heart jerked behind his rib cage at the pure emotion playing across her features. She dropped the weapon she'd offered him to her side as his request settled between them. Hesitation pulled her shoulders back as she prepared to run, but she couldn't deny the connection between them, what they'd shared since she'd answered his request to work this case. "Benning, I don't know what to say."

"Say you forgive yourself and that you've done

enough. Say you've saved enough lives to make up for the past, Ana." His voice grew stronger as he became more sure of himself than he'd ever been before. "You deserve to be with someone who loves you. You deserve a life that doesn't force you to detach yourself from everyone around you or that puts the people you care about at risk." He took her free hand in his. "I love you, and I want to build a life with you. I want you to be around for Owen and Olivia, and answer calls from the school and help them learn and grow, but…"

He dropped his chin to his chest as he realized what he had to ask her to do. She'd already sacrificed so much for him and his kids. How could he possibly ask her for more?

Her thumb smoothed over the side of his hand. "But what?"

"I need to know you won't hurt my kids the way you hurt me." He forced himself to look at her. His insecurity, anxiety, his need for her support, all of it bubbled to the surface as though he was still the same guy who'd just discovered the woman he'd been seeing had requested a transfer back to Washington. "That you won't leave without warning, that you won't cut yourself off from them if another victim turns up dead." Air caught in his throat. "I need you to quit the Tactical Crime Division."

She sucked in a deep breath, her hand shaking in his. Seconds ticked by, a tension-strained minute, before she finally opened her mouth to respond. She tugged her hand from his, that invisible guard slamming back into place as her shoulders stiffened. "You love me, but you want me to choose between you and your family or my duty to save lives."

"I know what I'm asking, and that this won't be an easy choice for you, but as much as I want you in our lives, I also have to think of Owen and Olivia. I wasn't strong enough to protect them from their abductor, and I won't submit them to another layer of trauma if I can prevent it." Benning read her decision as coldness swept over her expression, and the heat she'd ignited in his veins iced.

"You know why I do this job, why I push so hard. I can't just give that up, Benning." She took a step away from him, and the world threatened to rip out from under his feet. She was... She was choosing her job over him, over the twins. She was leaving. Again. "I'm sorry."

He nodded, not really knowing what he was agreeing to, but it didn't matter. He took the gun she'd offered, the steel heavy in his hands. They had a lead, and any ideas or fantasies about what kind of life he and Ana would have had to wait. "I guess that's it, then. When this is over, you'll go back to Knoxville, and I guess... I'll finally have the chance to move on with my life."

He maneuvered around her toward the bedroom door, the muscles in his jaw aching. Owen was still out there, and Benning wasn't going to stop looking until he found him. With or without Ana at his side.

Chapter Twelve

Over an acre of uneven green grass stretched between them and the light gray rambler on Maplewood Circle. Sevierville PD's SWAT team took position with a single wave of Ana's fingers toward the east side of the house as she, Agent JC Cantrell and Agent Evan Duran arced wide through a patch of trees at the opposite side of the property. No cars in the long driveway alongside the opposite end, nothing to suggest Claire Winston wasn't in Afghanistan with her military unit as Director Pembrook had reported, but that didn't mean someone wasn't home. Or waiting.

The low crackling of static from the device in her ear kept her focused, her movements steady despite the pain in her leg. She'd left Benning in the SUV for his own protection with an armed officer, but knowing he was on the other side of that signal still didn't settle her nerves. He'd asked her to give up a shot at redemption for the chance of being with him, with Owen and Olivia, a sacrifice he had no right to demand of her. She'd spent the past seven years trying to atone for her sins, and he just wanted her to walk away? To forget the people out there who needed her help?

She forced herself to focus. No matter what happened out here, he'd be safe. The wound in her chest ached as she pressed the stock of her rifle against her shoulder, but two bullets and a pane of broken glass wasn't going to stop her from finding Benning's son. Gravel crunched beneath her boots as she and her team slowly broke from the trees. "Our suspect has been trained in weapons and combat and has a .45 caliber Beretta M9 registered in her name. Eyes and ears open."

"Copy that, Ramirez," JC said.

Both JC and Evan had been military trained. If there was anyone from Tactical Crime Division she'd want at her side, it was them, but tension still crept across her shoulders as they closed in on the back door of the house. Red wood shudders groaned as a brush of wind barreled down the thin section of patio between the back door and the fence, and Ana raised her hand to signal the team to stop. The fence intersected with the back-east corner of the house, cutting off their access to the SWAT team and vice-versa. Her instincts screamed for her to get the hell out of there, but they hadn't gotten the chance to search the house yet. They had to keep moving. Owen's life depended on it. She motioned toward the back door. "Break it down."

Agent Evan Duran climbed the four stairs to the small back deck and tested the doorknob. With a single shake of his head, he adjusted his rifle, then slammed the heel of his foot near the knob. The crack of wood seemed overly loud as the wind died in an instant, and a shiver chased across Ana's shoulders. The door slammed into the wall behind it. Silence. No alarm. No explosion of gunfire. Nothing but the darkness waiting inside. Maybe Claire Winston really was serving with her unit overseas, but they had to be sure. Someone had stuffed Samantha Perry's killer's skull behind all that drywall, and the only motive that explained why was to hide something the killer hadn't wanted them to see.

Ana nodded to breach, taking up the rear behind her team, and swept into the house. It took a few seconds for her eyes to adjust to the low light, but it was clear nobody had been here in a while. Stale air dove deep into her lungs, a hint of moisture clinging to her face and neck. Dust floated in front of her face. She ran her finger through a thin layer coating the kitchen table to her left.

"Ana? You okay?" Benning's voice from her earpiece pierced through the steady pounding of her heart beating behind her ears. She could still smell him on her, that light hint of pine and man. They'd spent the night memorizing each other's bodies all over again, releasing the stress, fear and frustration of the past few days to the point neither of them could move. There'd been unspoken promises as she'd stared into his eyes and the world exploded around her, and she knew. Knew she'd failed in keeping emotional detachment from this case. Knew she wouldn't be able to walk away this time. Knew she couldn't spend the rest of her life living as a ghost. Knew she'd fallen in love with him and his fearless six-year-old in a matter of days. But then he'd asked her to sacrifice the one thing that'd given her purpose over the years, the one thing that'd kept her going and the guilt at bay. The only thing that could help her redeem herself. "Ana?"

Her throat tightened. She couldn't do it. She couldn't risk more victims for her own shot at happiness. She removed the device, dropped it on the floor and severed the connection between them with the heel of her boot.

JC and Evan took position on either side of the door leading into the basement, each of them waiting for her signal.

Ana raised her rifle. All her life this darkness—a physical hole in her chest—had followed her around after her sister had gone missing. She'd watched what that single event had done to her family, how her brothers vowed to uncover the truth, how her parents hadn't been able to live in the town they loved anymore. All that hurt, that pain, had been reignited the night her former partner had called to tell her he'd found Samantha Perry's body in that alley, and she'd only let that hole become bigger since. Now it didn't seem so deep, so…empty. And the credit had to go to Benning. To the way he cared for everyone else first, how he encouraged his kids to be the best versions of themselves without tearing them down, and how he was so determined to make her understand she deserved better. Deserved to be happy for once in her life. Shaking her head, Ana rested her cheek against the stock of her weapon. "Let's do this, guys. We've got a missing boy that needs to get home to his dad."

"On your signal." JC locked his hand on the doorknob.

She took another deep breath to settle her racing heart rate. "Go."

The door swung outward, and they all closed in. Their boots thudded on the unfinished stairs leading down into the house's basement as they cleared the corner and descended onto cement. Old two-by-fours had been stacked to the wall at their right, giving way to an underground cold storage stocked with cans, bags of flour and shelves of supplies.

Raising her weapon toward the ceiling, she flipped on her rifle's flashlight and skimmed the open cords and piping above. Cobwebs and dust glared back as they maneuvered down what she imagined would be a hallway if the basement had been finished, and into an open space. A single window allowed light to spill across the settling concrete, narrow cracks disappearing under a large piece of carpeting to one side. Only the carpet didn't look as level as it should be against a flat surface. It dipped toward the center.

Ana trained her flashlight on the spot and kicked at one edge. "I've got something over here."

Two other flashlight beams centered on the carpet at her feet as JC and Evan closed in. Crouching, she tugged the corner of the rough makeshift rug, then tossed it aside—and froze. Chunks of cement fell into the hollowed-out floor from the edges underneath the carpet. A hole, approximately six feet long, had been dug into the foundation. There, at the bottom, a plastic bag stained red remained. Flies buzzed past her ear, the slight hint of decomposition chasing back the scent of pine in her lungs. The plastic wasn't clear enough to see through, but she had a good idea of what was inside. Ana covered her mouth with the back of her hand, but nausea still churned.

"Lo que en infierno...?" Evan said. "What the hell is that?"

"My guess is the rest of Harold Wood." Ana's gut tightened. But why separate the skull from the body, and why dig it up after all this time? "We need to get forensics in here to confirm, but we have to clear the rest of the property first. Move."

"You don't have to tell me twice." JC slowly headed back the way they'd come.

Something wasn't right. Even if Claire Winston wasn't involved in Owen's kidnapping and serving with her unit overseas as she'd claimed, there was a strong connection between this case and the last case that'd brought Ana to Sevierville. Harold Wood. Pressure built behind her sternum as she caught sight of a small red light in one corner of the room, one she hadn't noticed before. The LED flashed once, then faster until she couldn't tell the difference between fluctuations. Warning launched her into JC's side. "Get down!"

Heat and debris seared across her vest as she took most of the blast to protect her teammate. She hit the ground hard face-first, her weapon pinned between her and concrete. Her ears rang as static crackled from the radio on Evan's chest, her vision darker around the edges. Stabbing pain kept her conscious. She tried to push up but couldn't get her balance. Where was JC? Evan? Were they injured? Alive? Her eyes watered as layers of dust filtered sunlight coming through the window. Someone had rigged an explosive to keep them from leaving with the remains. She coughed, sending more debris into the air. "Guys." No answer from her team. "Evan? JC?"

More static. Pressing one palm into the floor beside the hole, she was able to flip onto her back. Skeletal dust clung to the rafters and cords above. The explosive had to have been set underneath the rug. She must've triggered it when she'd uncovered the remains, and now Harold Wood had become more decoration than evidence.

Heavy footfalls vibrated through the floor as she gave in to the heaviness pulling her eyes closed. SWAT would've heard the explosion. She, JC and Evan would be okay. They'd be… She closed her eyes as water pounded onto her vest from above. Two steps. Three. Then silence as her ears stopped ringing. She struggled to open her eyes, the blurred outline of a man above her, and she gripped her weapon, only to have it taken from her. "You should've walked away when you had the chance, Agent Ramirez."

BENNING PUSHED OUT of the SUV as what felt like a punch of vibration shook the ground. "What the hell was that?"

"Sir, I need you to stay in the vehicle." The officer assigned to protect him raised his hands. Voices and static battled for dominance from the radio strapped to his chest. "SWAT's reporting an explosion from inside the house, possibly the basement."

An explosion? Blood drained from his face and neck. "Ana."

He shoved past the officer and bolted for the west side of the house toward the back, where Ana and her team had breached. Following the gravel driveway, he ignored the shouts telling him to stop and pumped his legs as hard as he could. The bullet wound in his shoulder screamed for him to slow down, but he pushed the pain to the back of his mind. If Ana had been down there when the explosion happened... His lungs burned with icy dread. He pounded up the four stairs of the back deck and raced inside the house. His heart threatened to beat out of his chest as he pushed deeper into the sparsely furnished home and caught sight of the open door leading down into the basement. White dust particles coated his neck and face as he neared. Cement? "Ana!"

No answer. He wasn't a federal agent, he wasn't SWAT and he didn't have a weapon or backup, but nothing was going to stop him from getting to her. He took each step one at a time. If he'd learned anything working in construction for the past two decades, it was that explosions affected more of a building than the blast radius. One wrong step and he could be added among any casualties. A crack of wood shot his heart into his throat a split second before footsteps reverberated above him on the main floor. SWAT had breached the house from the front. He had to move. The first chance they got, they'd secure him away from the scene, possibly in cuffs. Ana might not have that much time. His boots hit cement, dust clinging to his clothing and face. The cold storage straight ahead didn't look like it'd suffered any damage, and he followed the curve of the hallway around until he found the epicenter of the explosion.

A beam fell from the ceiling, wood on concrete loud in his ears, and he raised his hands to block the blast of dust coming straight at him. The unfinished door frame held strong against the explosion, but what he imagined used to be an open living space had been closed off by twisted ducting, broken plumbing and exposed wiring. Damn it. He had to get in there. Had to get to Ana. Water splattered against the floor, but he couldn't tell from where. It carved rivers around his boots to the drain where a bathroom would sit if the construction had been finished. At least the place wouldn't flood. Dust worked down into his lungs, and he coughed into the crease of his elbow. "Can anyone hear me?"

A groan broke through the rush of water, just on the other side of the ducting blocking his way into the room, and Benning shoved the metal shaft off to one side. The hole in his shoulder screamed, but after everything the Tactical Crime Division had done for him and his family, getting Ana and her team the help they needed was the only thing that mattered right then. The drain behind him was backing up, making it hard for his boots to get any leverage to move the piece of ducting. The groan he'd heard had been distantly male, which meant Ana hadn't heard him or she was unconscious, and this damn section of ducting was keeping him from getting to her. "Somebody shut that water off!"

Multiple sets of boots echoed off the unfinished stairs as SWAT descended into the basement. "You heard him! You, find the main water valve and shut it down. You two, get over there and help him get that debris out of the way. We've got agents in there."

Two armed SWAT members made quick work of clearing a path into the main room where the explosion had originated, and Benning hefted the last of the debris out of his way. "Holy hell."

Blood. A lot of it. His stomach wrenched as he homed in on the massive hole in the middle of the foundation. A bag had been torn to shreds by the blast, but he didn't have time to figure out what— or who—had been inside. Movement registered off to his left, and he caught sight of a boot pinned beneath more debris. His heart rocketed into his throat. Ana? Hauling more ducting and beams out of his way, he struggled to keep the panic clawing through him at bay. She'd already taken two bullets and a window pane through her femoral artery. If she'd been injured in the blast, how long before her body decided it'd had enough? "Ana. Talk to me. Tell me where you are."

Another groan cut through the patter of water on cement. Lifting a panel of drywall off the agent, Benning froze. Agent Duran. Dropping beside the hostage negotiator, he tried to plug the blood trickling from below Duran's vest with both hands and applied pressure. Pieces of concrete bit into his knees as he searched the rest of the scene. The sound of metal hitting cement caused his ears to ring as the other two members of SWAT cleared a path to another agent a few feet away. Agent Cantrell. No. No, no, no, no. She was here. She had to be. He turned back to Duran. "Where is she? Where's Ana?"

"The body…" Small muscles flexed in the agent's jaw as he tried lifting his head off the floor. "Rigged to blow."

"Body?" His pressure on Duran's wound faltered. The bag in the hole, the one covered in chunks of cement. The pounding at the base of his skull increased. "Who's body? Who was in the bag?"

"Harold... Wood." Sweat built along the hostage negotiator's hairline. "Someone unburied it from under the cement and... Ana shouted for us to get down." Wet coughing arced Agent Duran off the floor. The blast must've punctured a lung. "The bomb was a...distraction."

"What do you mean, a distraction?" Benning fought to catch his breath as a pair of EMTs stepped in to take control of the agent's injuries. He straightened, circling the area, searching every square inch of the space, under every piece of debris. EMTs pulled both Agents Cantrell and Duran from the scene on stretchers, but they still hadn't found Ana. The bomb was a distraction. A distraction from what? Running his hands through his hair, he ignored the thin layer of blood on his hands as the single window at one end of the room came into focus. "She's not here."

Ana wouldn't have left her team to bleed out. Wouldn't have left the scene of a crime without telling anyone. Especially if she'd been injured as badly—if not worse—than Cantrell and Duran. Distraction. He understood how explosives worked. Depending on the setup, whoever had set that charge would've had to have been within proximity to trigger the explosion. They would've needed to watch the house in case the Tactical Crime Division identified the skull he'd pulled from the construction site and needed to tie up loose ends. Ana would've known that, too. He didn't see any evidence the basement was being surveilled. Then again, there wasn't much of a basement left. Claire Winston—or whoever was responsible—could still be close if it had been triggered remotely. Had Ana realized the same and gone after that person? No. Cantrell and Duran barely survived that close-quarters blast. Ana wouldn't have been able to get out on her own, which meant someone had to have dragged her out.

Benning wound his way through the scene, back to the stairs leading to the main floor of the house, and out the way he'd come in. Crisp air picked up, and the hairs on the back of his neck rose on end. Thick trees lined the back of the property on the other side of the fence, leaving miles of open wilderness. Curling his fingers into his palms, he battled against the uncertainty threatening to break him. No new leads on Owen, and now Ana had gone missing. No. He wasn't going to lose them. He couldn't. Branches shifted with the wind and exposed a dark green structure set back about an acre behind the main property. Something he never would've seen if he hadn't still been standing on the back deck. Slats in the wooden fence swung loose with another gust, and he stepped down—and froze. A swipe of blood on one of the slats. Fresh from the looks of it. "She left a trail."

Or whoever'd taken her had.

SWAT and the rest of the Tactical Crime Division were focused on the scene, and Benning couldn't waste time trying to convince someone to follow his hunch. He had to go now. Kicking the bottom of the fence, he wrenched a few more slats loose until he could fit, and slid to the other side. Flakes worked down into his boots, but it'd be easy to avoid if he retraced the large set of footprints interrupting the smooth surface of recent snowfall. Warning exploded behind his sternum as he closed in on the seemingly unused structure ahead. Tractor storage? A door on one side had been left partially open. He pressed his back against the opposite door and twisted around to see inside the other. No movement. Nothing to make him think someone was inside, but the footprints—Ana's or the attacker's—had led straight to the garage.

Old hinges protested as he pried the door wider, and he stepped inside. Darkness bled around the edges of his vision before his senses adjusted. His exhales crystallized in front of his mouth, but something other than low temperatures chased a shiver down his spine. He slid one hand along the cold metal wall until he found a light switch, but flipping it on did nothing. Someone had fled from Claire Winston's house and come here. Why? As far as he could tell, the shed was empty, and there were no fresh tire tracks to suggest a vehicle had been waiting here.

Except...

Except the small LED light casting a red glow across the metal sheeting on either side of it hadn't been there when he'd come in. Benning hit the light switch again, and the light disappeared. His footsteps echoed off cold cement and thin metal walls as he stretched one hand above his head and ran it over where he'd noticed the light. There. Ripping the device from its position, he turned to face the light coming in through the doors. Severed wiring brushed against the palm of his hand, a small lens reflecting the sunlight. "A camera? Why would you need a camera in—"

The video from the shooter's phone. Owen had been crouched in a dark room like this. Alone, crying, scared. Benning spun around, fixating on the exact position his son would've been sitting for the camera to catch that angle of his face, and something inside him broke. He smoothed one hand over the cold flooring as he nearly crushed the camera with his other. The cement was still warm compared to the area around it. This was where they'd held his son. In a cold, barren tractor shed where no one would find him. Where they'd let him cry for hours with no one to tell him it'd be okay. Rage replaced the gut-wrenching desolation. He pocketed the camera and stood. "I'm coming for you, buddy. Both of you."

Chapter Thirteen

Her ears were still ringing.

She couldn't move her hands or legs, couldn't get enough air. It felt as though an elephant had sat on her chest and was refusing to move. She'd taken the brunt of the blast in Claire Winston's basement. She remembered that, but then…nothing. Her team had been there. JC and Evan. Were they okay? Had they gotten out alive? *Infierno.* It hurt to breathe. She must've cracked a—

"Please don't be dead," a small voice said.

Every cell in her body stilled, only the sound of a low humming audible over her uneven heartbeat. Ana struggled to open her eyes, met with only more darkness. Not a hospital. Tugging at her wrists, she battled gravity and a headache to pull her head off the floor of wherever she'd ended up. The floor underneath her was cold, but she wasn't alone. She could barely make out the shape of a small outline resting across her midsection. Her head fell back to the floor. The weight on her chest wasn't from an elephant. "I'm not dead. Are you?"

"No." The boy's voice shook. "But I'm cold and my tummy hurts. And I want to go home."

"My name is Ana." Relief coursed through her. He was alive. She'd found him. She pulled at the zip ties securing her wrists and ankles. Where the hell were they? Flashes of memory ignited in the front of her mind. The explosion had knocked her face-first onto the floor. There'd been water pounding down on her back, but over that, she'd heard footsteps. Then he'd been standing over her. The man who'd shoved her through the window at the safe house. Her head throbbed. He must've taken her from Claire Winston's basement somehow and brought her here. Wherever *here* was. Barely making out a row of shelving beside her as her vision adjusted, she swallowed the chemical burn at the back of her throat. Industrial cleaner? "Your daddy sent me to find you, Owen."

A combination of excitement and hope bled into his voice. "You know my dad?"

"Yeah." She nodded but wasn't sure he could even see the motion. "We're friends. He's been worried this entire time you've been gone, so he called me and asked me to help find you. I'm here to take you home."

Pain arced through her as the six-year-old tablet enthusiast with a pension for stealing cookies in the middle of the night pressed his hands into her side to sit up. "How are you going to do that with your hands and feet tied?"

"That's a good question." No windows. A slight hint of humidity in the air, like a basement. Bare cement bit into her elbows as she shifted enough to sit up against the metal shelving. There had to be something—anything—she could use to break these ties and figure out where their kidnapper had brought them. In an instant Owen had curled back into her side. If her hands had been restrained in front, she would've captured him inside the circle of her arms. But the best she could do was set her cheek against the top of his head. The odor of gasoline and dirt in his hair chased back the smell. "I don't know yet, but I'm sure we can figure something out. As long as we're together, we'll be okay. I promise."

Short hair bristled against her Kevlar vest, and she imagined he was nodding, but the tremors rolling through him said he didn't have much time. The boy was alive, but she had no idea what kind of circumstances he'd been held, if he'd been given food and water, been able to sleep. Setting her head back against the metal shelves, she stared up at the blackness above them. First things first, she had to get out of these ties, but she needed his help. She thought back to what Benning had told her about his son. "Okay, Owen, I need you to stay awake as long as you can, okay? Because we're going to play a game."

"What game?" he asked.

She had to keep him talking, keep him moving,

before the cold set in too deep, and he stopped fighting. "How about a treasure hunt? Do you like those?" He nodded against her vest again. "Great. First piece of treasure we need to find is my flashlight. Do you see where it's attached on my vest?"

In less than two breaths, he detached the flashlight and hit the power button. Bright light punctured through the blackness surrounding them, and for the first time, she was able to see him clearly. Dark smudges across his features highlighted crystal-clear blue eyes. Just like his father's. "I found it."

With one look this sweet boy had reminded her how tightly closed in on herself she'd become over the years—since Samantha Perry's body had been found—and how very exhausting it was to keep going. Cut off from everyone around her. There, but never committed. She'd been living, surviving by giving her body the basic needs that would keep it going, ensuring everyone she'd been assigned to find got their happily-ever-after, but that wasn't a life. Benning was right. She deserved more. She wanted more. She wanted…something for herself. Benning had tapped into the things she'd tried burying and exposed them for the world to see, and there'd been a sort of freedom in that. He'd broken her open and shown her what could be. What they could be. Together. If she only had the courage to give up her shot at redemption. But how long—how many lives— would it take to achieve it? How long did she expect to play hero without knowing an exact number of victims she would have to bring home to their families while she put off the chance of having a life of her own?

Ana studied Benning's son in the castoff from the flashlight's beam. There was a hole in the sleeve of his pajama shirt and not much color in his face, but otherwise he seemed unharmed, and that was what mattered. Tears burned in her eyes as pride transformed his features from hopeless to excitement. "Great work. You're really good at this game."

"What's next?" The tremors tensing his small muscles hadn't abated, even with him tucked into her side. Her breath materialized on the air. He'd been taken from his home—from Benning—in the middle of the night in his pajamas. No coat. No socks. Nothing to keep his body from dropping into hypothermia while he'd been held. They had to get out of here. Now. Before his organs started shutting down.

"Okay. Now we need to find something that can cut through these ties on my hands and feet. Shine the light over here." She pressed her heels into the floor to sit higher and twisted her head around to search the shelves. The flashlight beam wavered over the shelves filled with cleaning supplies, rolls of toilet paper, cleaning rags and paper towels for steel bathroom dispensers. No tools. Nothing that could cut through plastic. "I don't see anything, but that doesn't mean we've failed. Here, move over here. I don't want to accidentally hit you."

He did as asked, bringing the light back to her

as she rocked forward onto her knees and stood. Increasing the tension between her wrists, she bent forward slightly, then slammed her wrists against her lower back. Plastic cut into her skin, and she bit back a groan and tried again. Taking a deep breath, she kept her gaze on Owen's. If she couldn't get out of here, they were both going to die. Ana closed her eyes and slammed her wrists down one more time. Her arms shot out to the sides as the zip tie fell away.

"Whoa!" Owen's eyes widened in delight. "How did you do that?"

"My three older brothers made sure I knew how to escape any kind of situation when I was younger." Her stomach clenched as she thought back to the countless hours they'd spent in their family basement practicing escape tactics, and the reason why, but all of it had paid off. In this moment. Dropping into a fast squat, she smiled as the ties around her ankles snapped and she handed the plastic to Owen. "After we get you home, I'll teach you."

"Cool." He took the zip ties, then handed her the flashlight. "I'm going to tie up my sister and see how long it takes her to get out. She's always hiding my stuff in our fort."

"Yeah. I've been on the receiving end of that. Here, put these on." She pulled off her windbreaker, followed by the Kevlar vest, and unlaced her shoes to get to her socks. If it hadn't been for Olivia's interception of Harold Wood's skull, they never would've connected Owen's kidnapping to Claire Winston.

Although, it would've been nice to have known she'd taken it in the first place. Ana handed over her socks and helped Owen with the oversize windbreaker. Strapping her vest back into place, she ignored the slight chill on the air and tunneling deep into her bones. She'd give him everything she was wearing to ensure his body temperature came back up, but the best thing she could do for both of them right now was get the hell out of here. Ana used the flashlight to search the rest of the room. Shelves stocked with cleaning supplies, a few mops, brooms, a single drain in the center of the floor and a rolling bucket. It was a janitor's closet. But where? She tested the doorknob. Locked. But had she expected any differently? A large vent rained dust down from overhead as the air kicked on. "Here, hold the flashlight and point it toward this vent."

"Why?" he asked.

"Because I'm getting you out of here." Dragging the mop bucket from the corner, she centered it beneath the vent. She balanced on the cheap plastic, the bottom of the bucket threatening to cave in from her weight, and she stretched slowly toward the ceiling. Swiping her fingers along the edges, she found the single screw in each corner but couldn't get any of them to turn. Disbelief pierced through the small amount of hope that'd surfaced. The vent had been welded shut, and unless she found something to carve out the sealed edge, they were trapped. For as long as their kidnapper wanted.

The door swung open.

Ana jumped from the bucket, maneuvering herself in front of Owen as the man in the ski mask centered himself underneath the door frame. Her heart pounded loud behind her ears, every breath still strangled from the pressure of her cracked rib. "You."

"I was getting worried I'd packed too much explosive into the device under Harold Wood's remains." Pulling his gloves from his hands, the man in the mask widened his stance, as though expecting a challenge. "Don't get me wrong, I didn't want anyone to find him in Claire's basement or the skull behind that wall, Agent Ramirez, but I'm coming to realize it's going to take more than a window and a bomb to shake you from this case. But you've always been that way, haven't you? Like a pit bull with a bone. You just couldn't let it go, and well, neither could I. Now, here we are."

She pushed Owen behind her, ready to fight the bastard for however long it took to give the boy a chance to run. "What do you want?"

"The same thing I've wanted from the beginning." Their abductor reached for the mask covering his head and pulled the fabric free, and shock coursed through her as recognition flared. He closed the door behind him, closing off their only chance of escape. "To finish what I started."

THE FOOTPRINTS VANISHED once Benning reached the road. The SOB who'd taken his son could've gone

anywhere, could've had a car waiting, or been working with Claire Winston this entire time. One person to recover the skull, one to keep watch on Owen.
Hell. He clutched the camera he'd taken from the
tractor shed and spun around to search for a sign of
where the bastard might've gone. The signal on a
device like this couldn't have reached far. It wasn't
powerful enough. The kidnapper would've had to
remain within a few blocks, maybe a mile, in order
to access the surveillance feed. Damn it. That still
left a lot of options. Too many. "Come on."

There had to be something he could use, but the
spatters of blood had ended at the edge of the pavement. Right along with the trail. Agent Duran had
said the body in the hole in Claire Winston's basement had belonged to Samantha Perry's killer. Could
she have been involved from the start? In an effort
to find Samantha some semblance of justice, had it
been Claire's plan to leverage Benning's son, in return for the evidence she'd committed murder? He
searched every loose piece of gravel under his boots,
every tire tread imprinted in slush along the side of
the road. Nothing. Ana and Owen were gone.

Branches swayed behind him on a strong gust of
wind. He was a building inspector. Tracking killers and missing persons? This wasn't his world. He
hadn't been trained for this, and that inexperience
would keep him from finding two of the most important people in his life, but he couldn't give up.
Not when Ana had finally come back into his life,

when everything had started falling into place and they were so close to finding his son.

His stomach soured. He'd asked her to give up the only chance she had of forgiving herself for the sake of the twins, but faced with the possibility of losing her, of losing Owen, he knew he hadn't been thinking of anyone but himself. He'd asked her to sacrifice a significant part of her life in order to protect himself from getting hurt again. Damn it. He'd been an idiot. Ana wasn't just an agent. Helping those who couldn't help themselves made her into the woman he'd fallen in love with. Now she was gone. They had a real chance to make this work between them and the twins, but that wasn't going to happen if he couldn't get to her to tell her the truth. Guns, blood, fear... This was her world, but he'd become part of it the second he'd removed Harold Wood's skull from that construction site. He'd fallen in love with a dangerous woman determined to go to the ends of the earth to ensure he and his kids made it out alive, and he couldn't leave her out there alone. Benning curled his fingers around the camera in his palm. He was the one who'd put Owen and Olivia in danger in the first place and brought Ana into the investigation. He'd started this. He was sure as hell going to finish it. "Think, damn it."

All of this tied back to that case from seven years ago, and while he hadn't been involved, there'd been enough in the news and from conversations between him and Ana for him to fill in a timeline. Harold

Wood had been a model employee at Sevier County High School where both Samantha Perry and Claire Winston attended. Samantha had been well liked, a favorite of her teachers, a fast learner and dedicated to achieving valedictorian during her senior year. The perfect target. According to her best friend, Samantha could become friends with anyone, made sure to smile at the kids who sat alone at lunch, as well as the janitor who kept to himself most of the time. Harold Wood. Claire's statement after Samantha had gone missing had gone public after the girl's body had been found in that alley in Knoxville. Benning studied the spot where the footprints ended. What had she said? He closed his eyes. The girls had been halfway home in Claire's car when Samantha realized she'd forgotten a textbook she needed in order to study for a test the next day. Claire had driven them back and waited in the parking lot, but after more than thirty minutes, she went in to look for her friend. And never found her.

Goose bumps rose along his arms as another gust shuddered through the trees. He opened his eyes. The school. That was where all of this started that day seven years ago, and that was where it would end. He was sure of it. This entire investigation had linked back to Samantha Perry's disappearance, and the school would be within signal range to stream the footage from the camera in his hand. Whoever was behind this—whoever'd taken his son—would be there.

He jogged east down the long, winding road in the direction of the high school despite the pain arcing through his shoulder. He wouldn't give up on Ana. Not a chance in hell. Because when it came right down to it, she wouldn't give up on him or his family. She hadn't shared her secrets with anyone. Not her team. Not her boss. Only him. She'd punished herself for failing to bring down a killer—had walked out on him because of it—but he would spend the rest of his life trying to help her work through that pain to lighten her burden. As long as it took. She'd dedicated her life to taking care of so many others, always putting everyone else's needs ahead of her own, and it hadn't been fair of him to ask her to give that up. This was his chance to take care of her, to make it right. He didn't know what the future held for them—if they had one at all—but he'd sure as hell give it everything he had. Whether that meant him and the kids driving to Knoxville to see her or her coming to visit between cases, it didn't matter. As long as they were together.

Because he loved her.

The past didn't matter. He wanted her present, her future. Anything she would give him, Owen, Olivia and he would take. She'd been missing from his life for too long, had taken a piece of his soul with her when she'd run, and he had a chance to get it all back. He'd already lost her once. He wasn't going to let it happen again. "I'm coming, baby."

His muscles protested as he pushed himself

harder. The large white dome over the main building had been buried beneath several inches of snow, the grounds pure white. There were still a few cars in the main parking lot, and too many footprints for him to isolate the ones he'd followed from that tractor shed. Despite the personal nightmare tearing apart his family's life, students were still living out their lives by trying to survive math class. However, after more than one hundred school shootings across the country in the past year alone, security measures wouldn't allow anyone in the building without checking in with the office first. And police would've already been on location if the bastard had been dragging Owen behind him. So the man in the ski mask had to have gotten inside another way. Jogging along the east side of the structure, Benning kept his back to the light reddish-brown bricks. School had ended a few hours ago, most of the students and teachers off campus, but there was still a chance any one of them could be put in danger. He should've informed the rest of the Tactical Crime Division, only there hadn't been time. He was on his own.

Benning tested the door trying to blend in with the same color paint as the bricks around it at the back of the building. He'd gone to school here over twenty years ago but couldn't exactly remember what was on the other side of the barrier. The knob turned in his hand easily. Unlocked. His stomach clenched. This was it. They had to be here. He threw the heavy metal door out wide and rushed inside. In a single breath, the door slammed closed behind him on automatic hinges and cast him into darkness. His exhales echoed in the small space as he raised his hands out in front of him. No voices. No footsteps. Nothing but stale, humid air slipping through his fingers.

Sweat built along his spine despite the temperatures growing more frigid as he took the stairs one by one. The sound of his boots on cement broke through the groan of piping and electrical humming. The basement. Pushing his hair back behind his ears, he narrowed his gaze ahead as the stairs ended. His blood pumped hard at the base of his head as he pushed one foot in front of the other, slowly working down the long corridor stretched out in front of him. Every cell in his body vibrated with awareness. Every sound, every smell, every blink of the old fluorescent lighting at the other end of the hall. Cracks mapped out dendritic patterns across the cement, up the cinderblock walls and along the edge where the wall met the ceiling. A constant dripping ate away at his senses as he closed in on the end of the corridor.

They had to be here. Because if they weren't… No. There were no other options. He couldn't spend the rest of his life wondering what'd happened to his son and the love of his life. Couldn't live with the thought that he could've done more. The muscles in his jaw clenched hard. He'd seen what Ana had put herself through. Cutting herself off from her family, from the people who loved her, from feeling anything. He wouldn't do that to Olivia. This ended now.

A shadow darted across the wall ahead.

Benning froze. He hadn't been sleeping well, hadn't been taking as much care of himself as he should have since the twins had been abducted, and he'd been hit not once but twice in the back of the head over the past few days, but he hadn't imagined that. The hairs on the back of his neck stood on end. Warning slithered through him, and he stretched his hand out toward a supply shelf bolted into the wall to his right as he passed. Cold steel warmed in his hand as he gripped a crowbar. The weight of metal tugged on the stitches on his shoulder, but the pain wouldn't slow him down this time. There was too much at stake.

The shadowed outline of a man came into focus at the end of the corridor, but in the next second disappeared. A deep laugh echoed off the cinderblocks around him and settled in his gut, and Benning strengthened his hold on the crowbar. He wasn't alone down here. "I brought your camera back, you bastard."

Chapter Fourteen

Familiar dark eyes locked on hers, and she couldn't move. Couldn't think. All this time, it'd been him from the beginning? "You kidnapped Owen and Olivia. You attacked us at the safe house. You buried Harold Wood's body in Claire's basement. All of it. It was you. Not her."

Her partner when she'd first been assigned the Samantha Perry case.

Agent Ericson York.

It'd been years since they'd worked together, but this didn't make sense. He'd taken an oath to uphold the law and seen firsthand the kinds of monsters that were out there. Monsters like Harold Wood. Her fingers brushed against Owen's arm behind her as she cornered the boy as far from Ericson as she could. The theory Claire Winston had somehow found Harold Wood and gotten the justice for Samantha fizzled right in front of her. Claire had the means and motive to exact revenge, but the FBI hadn't been able to locate Wood for almost a decade. How would she have been so fortunate? The answer stood right in front of her. "Claire didn't kill Harold Wood. You did."

"That bastard deserved everything that came his way, Ramirez." Dark clothing hid mountains of muscles and determination Ana had already gone up against once. And lost. A high widow's peak reflected the light coming from the bare bulb above off Ericson's shorn head. They'd worked side by side, taking down the monsters after witnessing exactly what they were capable of, for years. She'd trusted him to have her back, and she'd had his. But after the Samantha Perry case, he'd gone dark. Left the FBI, wouldn't answer her calls, moved out of his apartment. Now she was the only thing standing between him and his determination to get away with murder. He tossed the mask to the floor near the drain, keeping his hands free for his next move. "You weren't there. You didn't have to see what he'd done to her. You were thirty miles away with that local contractor while I was left to clean up Harold Wood's mess." He took a single step forward, shortening the distance between them and the space she'd have to defend herself and Owen. Ericson's voice dropped into dangerous territory. "So yeah, I did whatever it took to hunt him down. I kept tabs on his sister in case he reached out for help. I sat on his apartment for months at a time. I busted anyone he'd go to for a fake ID because I knew he wasn't finished. You want to know how I finally found him, Ramirez? What he did to get himself caught?"

He took another step toward her, and her breath shuddered in her chest. The closet he'd held them in suddenly seemed so much smaller than it had a few minutes ago.

"The sick SOB had the nerve to go after Claire," he said. "He couldn't stop himself. Didn't matter how many agents and law enforcement organizations were out there looking for him. Harold Wood saw something he wanted, and he tried to take it. Only this time I wasn't going to let him get away with it." The scent of new car smell filled her lungs in the small space, exactly as she remembered from the safe house. He'd shoved her through a window, tried to kill Benning and his family. Had taken Owen and left him for days at a time to freeze and starve to death. This wasn't the agent she'd worked beside. The Ericson York she remembered wouldn't have gone after innocent children to solve a case. "You promised the Perry family we would find their daughter. Do you remember that? You let them down. You let the entire Bureau down. As far as I'm concerned, that makes you as guilty as Harold Wood ever was."

"We would've found him, Ericson. We were closing in, but instead you took the law into your own hands and murdered someone." She shook her head. "If anyone is as guilty as Harold Wood, it's not me. It's you. We swore to protect the innocent, but what you're doing—"

"That oath is nothing!" His exaggerated breath rose and collapsed his shoulders, and she turned to hug Owen closer. A crazed mania bled into the brown of his eyes for a few seconds before he seemed to get control over himself. "I spent over a decade with the FBI hunting the scum who get off on hurting people, only to watch them walk free on technicalities and plea deals." He rolled back his shoulders. "They deserve better than that, Ramirez. Samantha Perry deserved better than that, and I'm finally doing something about it."

The muscles down her spine hardened. She'd seen this side to her former partner before, the caged obsession he hadn't been able to keep locked away during interrogations and investigations, equal to the all-consuming fixation to destroy the criminals they brought to justice. Only, back then, she'd taken advantage of all that intensity, used it to break suspects, to get the confessions they needed, and do their jobs to protect the victims of the cases they took on. She'd never been the target, and now, she and the six-year-old boy behind her would be the ones standing in his way. But there was still a chance they could all get out of here alive.

"You're right. I wasn't there. I wasn't focused on the investigation and an innocent girl paid the price because of it, and I'm going to have to live with that the rest of my life." The hollowness in her chest throbbed. Ana shifted her weight between both feet but nothing could relieve the pressure. Because the truth was she and Ericson weren't so different. That case had changed them both for the worse, taken away any semblance of good in their lives, but she'd found her way back. To Benning. If he hadn't requested her to work this case, would she be the one standing on that side of the room in a few years? Less? Would she be the one hunting down the murderers who hadn't answered for their sins? "I've spent the past seven years punishing myself day in and day out by cutting myself off from the things and the people who made me happy because of that case. I overcommitted myself to the job thinking I could make up for my mistake, but there's nothing that will ever bring Samantha Perry back. No matter how many lives we save, Ericson, it's never going to be enough." Her mouth dried as her own words released the vise she'd carried all this time from around her heart. "Believe me, ignoring the grief and the anger only makes it worse. The only way we're going to get past this is if we take responsibility, find a way to move on and make the most of the life we have left."

"And leave behind all the innocent victims that killers like Harold Wood got their hands on?" he asked.

"What about Owen here? And Olivia? What about Jo West and Benning Reeves? Claire has been falsely suspected in helping you cover up Harold Wood's murder. What about those innocent lives?" she asked. "None of them deserve what you've done. Are you going to be able to live with that for the rest of your life?"

"I never meant for any of them to get tied up in

this." He cast his gaze to Owen behind her, his expression stoic, and a hint of the agent she'd known returned. The thick beard growth along his jaw and around his mouth aged him another ten years in an instant, and for a moment hope blossomed behind her sternum. He was telling the truth. He hadn't wanted any of this, but that didn't excuse him from what he'd done. "I knew the moment Benning Reeves called you, we'd be here. With you on one side and me on the other. Even after realizing you played your own part in what happened to Samantha Perry, this isn't what I wanted. I meant what I said before I pushed you through that window. You were always one of the good ones."

That small sense of hope shattered as tension flooded his shoulders and arms, and she leveled her chin with the floor. "So were you, but we both know I can't let you walk away from this, Ericson."

"I know. That's why this is going to hurt me more than it's going to hurt you." He arced his right arm back, and Ana reached for the first thing she could get her hands on along the shelves behind her and Owen.

Threading her fingers through the handle of a heavy gallon jug of bleach, she swung it into Ericson's head as hard as she could. Her former partner stumbled back into the door he'd come through a few minutes ago and it slammed open against the wall behind it. He didn't take long to recover. Rushing toward her, Owen's scream loud in her ears, Ericson swung his fist aimed at her face. She thrust his wrist out of alignment, barely missing the knuckles to her jaw, but the pain from the explosion slowed her down. She wasn't fast enough to block the second swing. Lightning struck behind her eyes as momentum threw her around into the shelves and pinned Owen between her and the metal. A kick to the back of her injured leg brought her down. She clutched onto the shelves for support but couldn't get to her feet in time.

"I'm sorry, Ramirez. I really am, but I can't let you take me in." Ericson closed in again, his massive outline blocking the light from the bulb hanging from the ceiling. "I'm not finished with what needs to be done."

"Leave her alone!" Owen rushed forward, beating his small fists against their kidnapper's leg, but it wouldn't be enough. Ana struggled to regain her balance as the boy did everything he could to protect her. "I'm going to tell my dad on you!"

With a single swipe of his hand, Ericson shoved Owen out of his way and into a collection of brooms and mops in the corner.

She pressed her weight into palms on one of the shelves and cringed as pain flared from the bullet wound in her chest. This was it. Her chance to get him back to Benning. Ana latched on to her former partner to keep his focus on her. "Owen, get out of here! Run!"

The six-year-old ran into the darkness on the other

side of the door just as Ericson's right hook slammed her into the floor. She bounced off the cement as his boot landed in her side, knocking the air from her lungs. Searing pain spread across her scalp as he fisted a handful of her hair and dragged her back into his chest. "It's just the two of us now, partner, and only one of us is getting out of here alive."

"You're right." She hauled her elbow back into his solar plexus. "And it's going to be me."

BENNING PUMPED HIS legs as fast as he could. He hadn't mistaken that scream. Ana had yelled for Owen to run. His son was here. He was alive. He turned another corner where he thought the bastard in the mask had disappeared but collided with a pint-size child instead. He hit the ground, the surprised scream coming from the boy barely registering over the crowbar pinging off cement. Owen. Locking his hands on his son before he could dart away, he pulled the boy to his chest. "Owen! Buddy, it's me. Daddy. I've got you. You're safe. I've got you."

He threaded one hand through his son's hair, holding on to him as hard as he could without crushing him.

"Daddy!" The six-year-old seemed so much smaller than he remembered then. More frail. His son shook in his arms. His skin was clammy with a thin sheen of sweat and cold as sobs racked through his tiny frame. The overwhelming relief Benning felt in that moment was all consuming. But in an instant

Owen pulled away, latching on to Benning's hand to try to get him to his feet. "Daddy, she's hurt. The man is hurting her. We have to help!"

Ana.

Dread clenched in his stomach. Unfiltered terror at the idea of leading Owen back toward his kidnapper flared hot under his skin. After everything they'd been through, the last thing he wanted right then was to let his son out of his sight, but Ana needed his help. She'd sacrificed herself before, to save him and Olivia at the safe house, and nearly died for it. He couldn't let her go through that again. "Owen, listen to me. I need you to find a spot to hide and stay there until I come get you."

"Don't leave me." Owen's voice slid into a notch above fear, and everything inside Benning urged him to get his son the hell out of there. But he couldn't leave Ana without backup. Not again. "I want to stay with you."

"I know you do, but I can't lose you again." He smoothed his hand over Owen's hair, the sickening scent of neglect heavy in his lungs. He had no idea what his son had gone through the past four days. How horribly he'd been treated, how many times he'd begged to go home without getting an answer from the darkness that'd surrounded him in that tractor shed. This wasn't a choice between his kids or the woman who'd risked her life for them. There was no choice. He'd left Ana behind once and she'd nearly died for it. He wouldn't make the same mistake twice. "I have to help Ana, but I can't do that if I'm worrying about you at the same time. So I need you to hide."

Owen nodded. "Okay."

"Good." Benning led his son back toward the same supply shelf he'd taken the crowbar from and hefted the boy onto the top. "Stay low. Don't make any noises. If you see someone coming, don't move, understand?"

"Yes." Owen slid onto his stomach and laid his head down.

"Good boy." Ruffling his son's hair, he took a step back to ensure he wouldn't be spotted the moment someone came around the corner into the corridor. "I love you, buddy. I'm coming back for you. I promise."

"Love you, too," Owen said. "Don't die, okay?"

"Okay." He couldn't fight the tug at one corner of his mouth. Collecting the crowbar from the floor where he'd dropped it after slamming into Owen, Benning retraced the boy's steps through a maze of corridors and open spaces containing old desks, a set of lockers and tables. His fingers ached as tension locked his hand around the only weapon he had against a trained professional determined to rip apart his entire life. His shallow breaths cut through the silence, mouth dry. He turned another corner.

And slowed as light spilled into the hallway from a single door up ahead. A body fell back onto the cement in the frame of light, a full head of long brown hair hiding her face, but instant recognition flooded through him. Ana. She wasn't moving, didn't even seem to breathe, and the world stopped. He wasn't too late. Couldn't be. Benning pressed his back into the wall behind him as he heel-toed closer. Blood dripped from the corner of her mouth, sliding along the column of her throat. Get up. She had to get up.

"You're only dragging out the inevitable, Ramirez." The man stepping out of the room and standing above her had the same voice of the one who'd interrogated him against that tree, but the mask was gone. Shorn hair, thick eyebrows arching over narrow eyes. Heavy facial hair had aged the man's face over the years, but Benning still recognized the agent Ana had been partnered with during the Samantha Perry case. Agent Ericson York. Benning had watched the man's press conferences, listened to his pleas for any witnesses to come forward. He'd been the face of the investigation. Now he seemed to be behind two kidnappings, attempted murder of a federal agent and the murder of Jo West.

"As long as you're…stuck here with me, you're not going…after Owen." Her laugh lifted her chest off the cement, followed by a deep, wet cough. Rolling onto her side, she pegged him with those hazel-green eyes, but kept moving to stand. "I'll drag… this out as long…as I have to."

Her attacker pulled a weapon from under his leather jacket at his low back and took aim at Ana.

"Let's see how long you last with a bullet between your eyes."

Benning raced to intercept. Gaining the agent's attention, he slid into the bastard's feet as Ericson turned the gun on him. The crowbar hit the floor. In his next breath, he hauled his boot up and kicked the weapon free from Ericson's hand. The gun vanished into the corner of the room, out of sight. The SOB who'd taken his son slammed a fist into the side of his head. Pain exploded through the left side of his face, and he stumbled back. Before the white lights behind his eyes cleared, a feminine growl filled his ears.

Ana launched herself at Ericson from behind, locking her forearm around his throat and pulling the agent away from Benning with a hard thrust. Ericson's hands went to her underarms a split second before he hauled her over his head and slammed her down onto her back. Her gasp of pain tunneled through the haze of both hits to his face, and Benning lunged for the crowbar. He swung as hard as he could, but Ana's former partner shot back on his heels and dodged the swipe and landed another shot to Benning's kidneys. He dropped to one knee as the pain shot through his side and down one leg, but Ana refused to go down.

She caught Ericson's wrist and wound it over her head before twisting around to crush his nose with the base of her other palm. His scream bubbled beneath a fresh wave of blood. Taking advantage as he stumbled back, she kicked him square in the chest. He hit the floor, a groan slipping past the former agent's lips.

She stood over Ericson, every bit the woman Benning had fallen in love with. Strong, protective, determined. His. Blood had already started drying along her face and neck. Swiping the back of her hand across her mouth, she swayed slightly as Benning got to his feet. "You can try to kill me as many times as you want and threaten to hurt the people I love, Ericson, but it's not going to change what happened to Samantha Perry, what you've done, or make up for the people you've hurt." Her voice shook as though her throat had tightened, and she relaxed her fists at her sides. "I'm sorry I wasn't as focused on the case as I should've been and an innocent girl died. I'm sorry I wasn't there for you after you found her body in that alley and that I didn't have the courage to make it to her funeral, and I'm sorry that you think this is the only way to bring Samantha justice." She shook her head. "But I've punished myself long enough. Now it's your turn."

The air rushed from his lungs. He couldn't speak. Couldn't even breathe. She'd done it. She'd finally forgiven herself. The tension in Benning's shoulders drained, and the pressure around his wound ebbed. Damn, he loved this woman. No matter how well he thought he knew her, she'd hit him with another surprise, and he only hoped he and the twins would be able to keep up with her when all of this was over. If she'd forgive him.

"You think you've paid for what you've done because you can admit you made a mistake?" Ericson spit a mouthful of blood off to his right, then recentered his focus on Ana, a cruel smile contorting his mouth. Sweat slipped down the man's temples, his chest rising and falling with shallow breaths. "You haven't even begun to pay, Ramirez."

Dim lighting reflected off a piece of metal in Ericson's hand as the bastard shot to his feet, and Benning lunged.

"Ana!" He collided with her former partner but came up short from tackling Ericson to the floor. The world threatened to drop right out from under his feet as screaming pain slashed through his gut. One second. Two. He stumbled back. Confusion built a wall between rational thought and the fact the blade had embedded deep into his body. Nausea churned in his stomach as Benning fell to both knees, dizziness throwing him off balance. His head felt heavy, but he somehow managed to level his gaze with Ericson's.

"Now you've paid." Ana's partner pulled the blade free, his expression smooth. As though he'd done this a hundred times and was prepared to do it a hundred more.

"No!" Ana shot forward, hiking her shoulder into Ericson's midsection and hefting him off the ground before she slammed him back into the nearest wall. Fists connected with bone, groans and blood cutting through the air as the woman he'd fallen for fought with everything she had left to protect him.

The gun. Benning could make out the grip highlighted beneath a pulsing fluorescent tube above. He clamped a hand over the stab wound in his gut, blood slipping through his fingers. Locking his jaw against the agony, he forced himself to his feet and stumbled forward to grab it. The weight felt solid in his hand as he turned and took aim. "Stay the hell away from my family."

Ericson positioned Ana in front of him as a human shield. The former agent's dark gaze cut to Benning, and dread curdled in his stomach. "I can kill her faster than you can take that shot, Mr. Reeves. Are you willing to take that chance?"

"She would do the same for me." Benning pulled the trigger.

Chapter Fifteen

It was over.

Red and blue patrol lights skimmed across her vision as Ana studied the scene from her position in the ambulance. Officers and emergency personnel almost seemed to move in slow motion, the strong thud of her heart beating at the base of her skull. There, in the middle of it all, Benning sat with his son on the back of another ambulance as snow fell across the parking lot. The man who'd risked everything that mattered to him in order to find her, and nearly died from a stab wound in the process.

Pressure built behind her rib cage, but not from the two broken ribs she'd cracked after the explosion in Claire Winston's basement. No. For the first time she could remember, she hadn't been the only one fighting. He'd fought Ericson York with her, for her. From the internal desolate landscape she'd created by detaching herself from everyone around her, he'd nurtured an ember and turned it into a wildfire. He'd shown her how to hurt, how to bleed, how to heal and how to feel again. None of which she could've done without him.

The Sevier County medical examiner and her assistant led the charge with Ericson York's body sealed into a dark bag on the gurney behind them, and her heart jerked in her chest. Her former partner had been a good agent, one of the best she'd worked with before transferring back to DC, then into the Tactical Crime Division, but neither of them had handled the repercussions of the Samantha Perry case well. The only difference between the paths they'd chosen had been that small piece of her that'd belonged to Benning Reeves the day she'd met him, and she'd never forget that.

Brilliant blue eyes settled on her as Benning recounted his statement to the Sevierville PD officer at his side, chasing back the nightmare of the past few hours. Owen was alive. Dehydrated, bruised, starved, but alive. She hadn't failed this time, and she realized Benning had been right from the beginning. Isolating herself from the people who cared about her—from the victims of her cases—didn't make her a better investigator. The detachment she'd relied on for so long had merely been a crutch to try to ebb the punishing guilt she'd taken on once Samantha's body had been found in that alley. A guilt that still weighed on her chest. Not as heavy, but there. She'd meant what she'd said to Ericson before he'd tried to kill her the second—third?—time. There was no magical number of lives saved or criminals punished to ease the blame they carried. The only way she was going to get past what'd happened on that case was to accept she'd done enough, but seven years of punishment wouldn't disappear overnight. It'd take time, support and help. Benning smiled at her from where EMTs stitched his wound, with Owen squished right alongside him. Luckily, she had all the support she'd need.

"I can see you didn't take my advice to be careful." Director Jill Pembrook leaned her shoulder against the back door of the ambulance, gray hair tied back in a severe bun that reflected the steel resolve inside. "What was it, two gunshot wounds, a pane of glass through your leg and a broken rib all within the span of four days?"

"Two ribs, and don't forget my broken finger, too." Ana pressed her palms into the gurney mattress in an attempt to sit higher when faced with her boss, but whatever the EMTs had given her to manage the pain hadn't kicked in yet. Pain shot through her midsection, and she pressed the crown of her head against the flat pillow as hard as she could to keep from groaning aloud. The fight with Ericson had been the most brutal battle not only for her life but also Benning's, Olivia's and Owen's, as well. She would've done anything—sustained anything—to make sure they'd made it out of this investigation alive. Because she loved them, all of them, as though they'd always been part of her life. Always been hers. She wanted to keep it that way, to wake up beside Benning every morning and fall asleep beside him every night, to respond to calls from the school when Olivia brought another dead animal to autopsy in the school's science lab, to brush the cookie crumbs out of Owen's bed before he went to sleep at night and compete with him on his newest game obsession. She wanted it all. The good parts and the messy parts, but she wasn't finished saving lives, either, and she wasn't going to let the director bench her because she hadn't followed Pembrook's orders to not let her emotions get in the way of doing her job. Swallowing through the tightness in her throat, she curled her uninjured hand into a fist to distract herself from the pain. "Do you have an update on JC and Evan yet?"

"Agent Cantrell sustained a mild concussion when the explosive went off but is expected to return to the field in a few days. Agent Duran, on the other hand, is currently in surgery to remove a piece of shrapnel from his side. He'll be out for longer, but his prognosis is looking good." Pembrook folded her arms over her pressed blazer and crisp white shirt, her expression controlled. "From what they've been able to tell me, they wouldn't have made it out of that basement alive if it hadn't been for Mr. Reeves disobeying SWAT's orders to stay away from the scene and risking his life so he could get to you." A hint of a smile pulled at one edge of the director's mouth, and Pembrook relaxed her hands to her sides as she straightened. "You're both idiots, but you obviously deserve each other. In any case, I expect you back on your feet and in the field as soon as possible, Agent Ramirez. The people we help still need you."

"Yes, ma'am." Ana rolled her lips between her teeth and bit down to fight back her own smile as Director Pembrook headed toward a beautiful African American woman dressed in military fatigues behind the perimeter of yellow crime scene tape.

Her smile slipped. Claire Winston. It'd been seven years since Ana had been face-to-face with Samantha Perry's best friend, but she would've recognized her at any age. Nausea worked through her. Ericson York had forced that poor woman to relive the nightmare of losing her closest friend so violently when he'd left one Libra charm on Benning's property and the other inside Harold Wood's mouth. *Infierno*, he'd even buried the rest of the killer's body in Claire's basement as some sick token of pride. But… that still didn't answer the question of why Ericson had removed Harold Wood's skull and hidden it separately from the body. Claire stretched her right hand to meet the director's in a handshake, and Ana narrowed her gaze on the woman's wrist.

A hint of a silver bracelet glimmered under the aura of patrol lights.

No charm.

Hadn't Claire told the director over the phone she still had her charm and wore the bracelet off shift while on tour? So then why wouldn't she be wearing it now?

"Tell me you're okay, and I won't have to shoot

anyone else tonight." Benning slid into her peripheral vision, Owen petting one of the canine units with another officer a few feet away.

"Help me up," she said.

"What?" Disbelief widened his eyes at the edges.

"Claire Winston isn't wearing her charm, Benning." Ana kept her voice low as she scooted down the length of the gurney toward the end. She slipped from the ambulance, relying on his support to stay on her feet. "Why would she tell the director otherwise unless she didn't want one of the charms we found during the investigation to be connected back to her?"

He searched the scene until his attention landed on Director Pembrook and the woman in fatigues near the perimeter. Turning back to her, he clamped his hand into hers and pulled her into his side. "You think she and Ericson were working together."

"Ericson told me Harold Wood made the mistake of going after Claire." She strengthened her hold around his hand as she studied the exchange between Pembrook and Claire Winston. "It wouldn't be a stretch to believe Claire might've helped get rid of the evidence once she learned she'd become Wood's next target. Why else would Ericson use her basement to hide the body?"

He kept his voice low. "Maybe to frame her in case he was caught."

"Ericson saved her life. He wouldn't have implicated her for a murder he was proud he'd committed, and he wouldn't give her up if she'd been involved in Owen's kidnapping, either." She shook her head. "Despite how far gone he'd become, he cared about her enough to make sure Harold Wood never got his hands on her."

"Then how do you prove she was involved?" he asked.

"I need to see Ericson's gun." Within minutes, Sevierville PD handed her the bagged weapon Benning had used to shoot her former partner and stop a killer, effectively saving her—and so many others. Releasing her grip on Benning, she turned the evidence over in her hand, the plastic sticking to the tips of her fingers. "This is a Glock 22, which shoots .40 caliber rounds, standard issue for FBI agents. Harold Wood was killed with a .45. The same caliber that would fire from the Beretta M9 registered in Claire Winston's name." The air rushed from her lungs as the pieces of the puzzle fell into place. "She did it. She's the one who killed Harold Wood, and Ericson hid the proof on the construction site in case the body was found. He tried to take the fall for her, and when you found the skull, he abducted Owen and Olivia to force you to give it back."

"Why would he take the fall for her?" Benning asked.

Claire Winston's dark, watery gaze followed the ME's movements as she loaded the bag with Ericson's body sealed inside, then rose to meet Ana's.

In an instant she knew the answer. "Ericson

blamed himself as much as anyone else for what happened to Samantha Perry. I think he believed protecting Claire was how he was going to finally redeem himself."

The confidence in Claire's expression bled to fear a split second before the woman ran from the scene. Only she didn't make it far. Without hesitation, Director Pembrook ordered officers to close off her escape, and Claire Winston raised her hands in surrender.

"You don't have to do this," she said. "The doctor said I'm fine on my own as long as I take it slow."

"That is in no way what she said. That's what you wanted to hear." But that wasn't the only reason he'd convinced her to recover in Sevierville instead of Knoxville. He'd almost lost her. Twice. Right along with the two most important humans in his life, who, he could see through the front window, were currently jumping up and down with excitement. His in-laws waved from behind Owen and Olivia before giving the twins each a hug and heading for the back door, which would take them to their pickup at the side of the house.

Maybe he hadn't chosen the right location for Ana to recover from her injuries, but he couldn't turn back now. He'd already informed the twins of his plan. Any deviation would only throw him into a world of whining and questions. He brushed his fingers against her low back as she stepped over the threshold to assure her he was there if she fell, but he knew without a doubt she wouldn't let things get that far. "I know exactly how long you'll rest before you try to convince the director you're ready for field work. You're staying here where I can keep an eye on you."

She slowed before reaching the entryway, those mesmerizing hazel-green eyes dark with suspicion. One hand tightened on the single crutch supporting her beneath her arm. "You don't trust me."

"With my life, yes. With your own, no." Staying close as she navigated slippery terrain on her way into the house—unassisted—Benning swung the front door open to clear her path and immediately held out one hand, palm forward, to stave off the twins from tackling her to the floor.

Owen and Olivia bounced in place, their grins bigger than he'd seen them in a long time as Ana stepped into the house. Over the past few days, he'd struggled to get their lives back to normal, but so much had changed. Owen had spent two days in the hospital fighting off dehydration and pneumonia but was acting more himself a little bit more every day, aside from the apparent break he was taking from his tablet, which Benning wouldn't complain about. Olivia had moved into sleeping in her brother's room, to make sure no one would take him from her. His heart had nearly broken all over again when she'd admitted how scared she'd been for her twin. But Owen was home now. They were safe, but Benning wouldn't be pulling any more skulls off construction sites anytime soon. As for Benning... Well, the biggest change for him was the woman insisting she could get herself into the house in a timely manner.

Ana's laugh cut through the off-the-charts energy emanating from the kids, but he couldn't blame them for not being able to hold back. He was just as excited—and nervous—for what came next. Only difference was he had more control over his body, and emotions and pretty much everything else. Except when it came to Ana Sofia Ramirez. "You sure you're up for this? I'm pretty stubborn, but those faces will knock me down with one hit. It's going to be chaos. I'm going to be giving them everything they ask for while I'm here."

"I think I'm up for the challenge." He turned toward the twins to distract himself from the heat climbing up his neck and into his face. "Why don't you guys take Ana to see what you made for her while she was in the hospital."

"It's not another skull, is it? Or a foot or something? I don't think I could take any more body parts right now." She leaned heavier into her crutch as Benning moved to close the front door behind them, then pulled back before the stampede of six-year-olds racing toward their rooms ran her over. Turning her gaze up to meet his, she silently questioned his motives.

"Guess they're excited." He motioned her to lead and followed close on her heels, head down to avoid eye contact. Every cell in his body rose in awareness as she limped along ahead of him down the hall, but he didn't have the capacity to overthink it as they entered Olivia's room.

Ana froze, the muscles down her spine pulling her shoulders tight. "What is this?"

Maneuvering to her side, Benning took in the sight of Owen and Olivia standing at the center of her room. In the middle of the crime scene they'd created together. After convincing one of the agents on Ana's team to hand over a brand-new roll of crime scene tape, his daughter had gone overboard with decorating her room until the pink paint faded into the background. But more horrifyingly cute was the white chalk outline Olivia had traced around her brother on the blue tarp from one of his inspection sites. Along with evidence markers, thinned out ketchup for blood, one of Olivia's favorite books, Owen's tablet, a hammer and a small velvet black box near evidence marker number three. "I know it seems terrifying, but they wanted to plan the whole thing and make sure a little bit of each of us was in there. Hence the book, tablet and hammer."

"I see. Olivia is the book, Owen is the tablet and you're the hammer?" She nodded slowly, taking it all in, but he couldn't read her expression. Cocking her head to one side, she narrowed her gaze. "And am I represented by the dead man in the middle or the blood?"

He pointed to the black velvet box off to one side. "I think that is supposed to be for you."

Owen collected the box from the floor and tipped the lid back on its gold hinges. Stepping near the perimeter of the scene, he stared up at Ana with a whole other level of excitement inching his smile wide. "Will you marry us, Ana?"

"Please?" Olivia asked. "We want you to stay. Forever."

The rush of air escaping from between Ana's lips cut through the hard beat of his heart behind his ears. She wiped the tears streaming down her cheeks with the back of her hand as another laugh escaped her control. Balancing the crutch under her arm, she sank a bit deeper on her uninjured leg to take the box from Owen. She turned toward Benning.

"I know I asked you to give up working for TCD to protect the kids, but it wasn't fair and it wasn't my place." He removed the ring from the box, the round diamond set in the platinum band strong enough to sustain any damage accrued during her future investigations. "I realized too late I was protecting myself. I wanted a promise you wouldn't disappear when the case was over, but asking you to stop helping people in need is like asking you to stop being the woman I fell in love with. And I love you just the way you are. I always have. Ana Sofia Ramirez—" he dropped to one knee, ignoring whatever sludge he'd just knelt in and slipped the ring onto her finger "—will you marry me?"

She smoothed her thumb across his bottom lip, the diamond sparkling from the low light coming through Olivia's window. "I told you I can't say no to those faces."

"Is that a yes, then?" he asked.

"Yes!" She tilted her head up to kiss him as he stood, and the excited screams from his kids fell into the back of his mind. Right then, there was only Ana. His strong, beautiful, determined FBI agent who hadn't just saved his kids' lives but completed his. "I love you. I've always loved you. You've always owned this part of me, and I know without a doubt you're the reason I didn't follow in Ericson's footsteps, Benning."

"I love you." He framed his hands around her face and kissed her again with everything he had. "And I'm always here for you. No matter what. But given your choice of career and the fact we have two humans to watch out for together, I think it's time I learned how to properly use a gun."

"Ewww." The tandem protest from Owen and Olivia cut through the heat searing across his skin where Ana touched him.

He laughed.

"This is only the beginning. It's going to get worse. Day. Night. In the bathroom. They're everywhere." His heart squeezed as she stared up at him with that gut-wrenching smile. Benning tightened his hold on her, a promise to have each other's backs.

Forever. "Are you ready for your next assignment, Agent Ramirez?"

She studied the scene the twins had made in Olivia's bedroom, then faced him again. "I think I'm up for the challenge."

* * * * *

COMING NEXT MONTH FROM

(H) HARLEQUIN
INTRIGUE

Available June 16, 2020

#1935 DOUBLE ACTION DEPUTY
Cardwell Ranch: Montana Legacy • by B.J. Daniels
When Montana deputy marshal Brick Savage asks homicide detective Maureen Mortensen to help him find the person who destroyed her family, she quickly accepts his offer. But as the stakes rise and they get closer than they ever expected, can they find the killer before they become targets?

#1936 RUNNING OUT OF TIME
Tactical Crime Division • by Cindi Myers
To find out who poisoned some medications, two TCD agents go undercover and infiltrate the company posing as a married couple. But as soon as Jace Cantrell and Laura Smith arrive at Stroud Pharmaceuticals, someone ups the ante by planting explosives in their midst.

#1937 CHAIN OF CUSTODY
Holding the Line • by Carol Ericson
When a baby lands on border patrol agent Nash Dillon's doorstep, Emily Lang, an undercover investigator posing as a nanny, comes to his rescue. But once he discovers why Emily is really there—and that both her and the baby's life are in danger—he'll unleash every skill in his arsenal to keep them out of harm's way.

#1938 BADLANDS BEWARE
A Badlands Cops Novel • by Nicole Helm
When Detective Tucker Wyatt is sent to protect Rachel Knight from her father's enemies, neither of them realizes exactly how much danger she's in. As she starts making connections between her father's past and a current disappearance, she's suddenly under attack from all sides.

#1939 A DESPERATE SEARCH
An Echo Lake Novel • by Amanda Stevens
Detective Adam Thayer is devastated when he fails to save his friend. But a series of clues brings Adam to coroner Nikki Dresden, who's eager to determine if one of the town's most beloved citizens was murdered. They must work together to unravel a deadly web of lies and greed...or die trying.

#1940 WITNESS ON THE RUN
by Cassie Miles
WITSEC's Alyssa Bailey is nearly attacked until investigator Rafe Fournier comes to her defense. Even so, Alyssa is unsure of who she can trust thanks to gaps in her memory. Racing to escape whoever has discovered her whereabouts, they soon learn what truths hide in the past.

YOU CAN FIND MORE INFORMATION ON UPCOMING HARLEQUIN TITLES, FREE EXCERPTS AND MORE AT HARLEQUIN.COM.

HICNM0620

After very little sleep and an early call from his father the next
morning, Brick dressed in his uniform and drove down to the law
enforcement building. He was hoping that this would be the day
that his father, Marshal Hud Savage, told him he would finally be
on active duty. He couldn't wait to get his teeth into something, a
real investigation. After finding that woman last night, he wanted
more than anything to be the one to get her justice.

"Come in and close the door," his father said before motioning
him into a chair across from his desk.

"Is this about the woman I encountered last night?" he asked
as he removed his Stetson and dropped into a chair across from his
father. He'd stayed at the hospital until the doctor had sent him
home. When he called this morning, he'd been told that the woman
appeared to be in a catatonic state and was unresponsive.

"We have a name on your Jane Doe," his father said now.
"Natalie Berkshire."

Brick frowned. The name sounded vaguely familiar. But that
wasn't what surprised him. "Already? Her fingerprints?"

Hud nodded and slid a copy of the *Billings Gazette* toward him.
He picked it up and saw the headline sprawled across the front
page, "Alleged Infant Killer Released for Lack of Evidence." The
newspaper was two weeks old.

HIEXP0620

Brick felt a jolt rock him back in his chair. "She's that woman?" He couldn't help his shock. He thought of the terrified woman who'd crossed in front of his truck last night. She was nothing like the woman he remembered seeing on television coming out of the law enforcement building in Billings after being released.

"I don't know what to say." Nor did he know what to think. The woman he'd found had definitely been victimized. He thought he'd saved her. He'd been hell-bent on getting her justice. With his Stetson balanced on his knee, he raked his fingers through his hair.

"I'm trying to make sense of this, as well," his father said. "Since her release, more evidence had come out in former cases. She's now wanted for questioning in more deaths of patients who'd been under her care from not just Montana. Apparently, the moment she was released, she disappeared. Billings PD checked her apartment. It appeared that she'd left in a hurry and hasn't been seen since."

"Until last night when she stumbled in front of my pickup," Brick said. "You think she's been held captive all this time?"

"Looks that way," Hud said. "We found her older-model sedan parked behind the convenience store down on Highway 191. We're assuming she'd stopped for gas. The attendant who was on duty recognized her from a photo. She remembered seeing Natalie at the gas pumps and thinking she looked familiar but couldn't place her at the time. The attendant said a large motor home pulled in and she lost sight of her and didn't see her again."

"When was this?" Brick asked.

"Two weeks ago. Both the back seat and the trunk of her car were full of her belongings."

"So she was running away when she was abducted." Brick couldn't really blame her. "After all the bad publicity, I can see where she couldn't stay in Billings. But taking off like that makes her either look guilty—or scared."

"Or both."

Don't miss
Double Action Deputy *by B.J. Daniels,*
available July 2020 wherever
Harlequin Intrigue books and ebooks are sold.

Harlequin.com

HIEXP0620

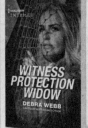

Don't miss the second book in the exciting Lone Star Ridge series from *USA TODAY* bestselling author

DELORES FOSSEN.

They've got each other—and a whole lot of trouble.

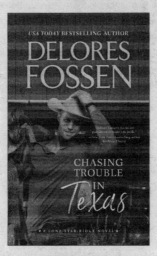

"Fossen creates sexy cowboys and fast moving plots that will take your breath away."
—Lori Wilde, *New York Times* bestselling author

Order your copy today!

PHDFBPA0620R

Love Harlequin romance?

DISCOVER.

Be the first to find out about promotions,
news and exclusive content!

Facebook.com/HarlequinBooks

Twitter.com/HarlequinBooks

Instagram.com/HarlequinBooks

Pinterest.com/HarlequinBooks

ReaderService.com

EXPLORE.

Sign up for the Harlequin e-newsletter and
download a free book from any series at
TryHarlequin.com

CONNECT.

Join our Harlequin community to
share your thoughts and connect
with other romance readers!
Facebook.com/groups/HarlequinConnection

HSOCIAL2020